The bad guys are after a hidden fortune that belongs to Flynn O'Mara's dying father—they think Tara can use her psychic powers to find it for them. She'll need plenty of help from her spirit friends if she and Flynn are going to get out of this trouble alive.

"Look out!" Tara screamed, as the sports car spun toward them.

The car hit them twice—first on the driver's side fender, then as Flynn's car started to spin, again on the back bumper.

"Hold on!" Flynn yelled, as their car flipped once, then went airborne, over the guard rail, and into Boomer Lake.

Tara came to as the car was sinking nose first into the water and quickly unbuckled her seat belt. If they were going to survive, they would have to get themselves out.

"Flynn! Unbuckle your seatbelt. I'm going to roll down the windows so we can swim out."

Then she saw Flynn, unconscious and slumped over the steering wheel. Frantically, she unbuckled his belt and tried to pull him toward her, but the steering wheel was too tight against his chest.

"I can't breathe," he groaned. "Help me, Tara, help me."

Tara began screaming at Flynn, begging him to move as the water rushed up to their chests—then their necks. She was holding Flynn's face out of the water, pushing him as far up as she could until their heads were touching the roof of the car. She couldn't believe this was happening. It was just like her dream. They were going to die. Where was her backup when she needed them?

"Millicent! Henry! Uncle Pat! Someone! Anyone! Help! Help!"

Seconds later, the water was over their heads.

Lunatic Revenge

Book three of the *Lunatic Life* Series

by

Sharon Sala

Bell Bridge Books

Bell Bridge Books
PO BOX 300921
Memphis, TN 38130
Print ISBN: 978-1-61194-179-1

Bell Bridge Books is an Imprint of BelleBooks, Inc.

We at BelleBooks enjoy hearing from readers.
Visit our websites – www.BelleBooks.com and
www.BellBridgeBooks.com.

10 9 8 7 6 5 4 3 2 1

Cover design: Debra Dixon
Interior design: Hank Smith
Photo credits:
Cover Art © Christine Griffin
Girl (manipulated) © Robert Clay | Dreamstime.com
Tornado and road © Victor Zastol`skiy | Dreamstime.com

:Lrl:01:

Also By Sharon Sala
From Bell Bridge Books:

My Lunatic Life

The Lunatic Detective

and

The Boarding House

Chapter One

"I can't breathe. Help me, Tara, help me."

More water was coming into the car now, creeping up their waists, to their chests, then their necks. Tara was holding up Flynn's head, but it wasn't the water that was restricting his breath, it was the broken rib that had punctured one of his lungs.

Tara couldn't believe this was happening, and that she was going to die before she had a chance to grow up.

Where was her backup when she needed them?

Millicent! Henry! Uncle Pat! Someone! Anyone! Help! Help!

Seconds later, the water was over their heads.

The alarm went off.

Tara woke with jerk and then flew out of bed before she realized where she was. She took a deep breath, still locked into the dream that she and Flynn had been drowning.

"OMG, that was seriously wack."

She sank back onto the side of the bed, and didn't realize until she turned off the alarm that it was raining. That explained the water dream, but not why she had seen her and her boyfriend in danger.

For most people, assuming a dream had real meaning would have been silly, but Tara wasn't like everyone else. Not only did she see ghosts, but she was psychic, too. It made every day of her life a challenge. What bothered her now was that for some time she'd felt something dark hanging around Flynn. She just couldn't get a handle on whether it was a dark spirit, or a living, breathing baddy?

She'd talked to Millicent and Henry, the two ghosts who lived with her and her Uncle Pat, but for whatever reason they'd been mum. Either that meant she was on the wrong track, or they weren't supposed to tell. There were rules where they came from about what they could and couldn't reveal—stuff that Tara didn't fully understand.

So it was raining, which meant the walk to school would suck eggs. Still in a bad mood from the dream, Tara made a quick trip to the bathroom and then headed for the kitchen to start the coffee for her uncle. With this weather, his day was going to be miserable too, reading meters for the City of Stillwater.

She could hear voices as she headed down the hall and, when she reached the living room, realized the television was on. Uncle Pat must already be up, only when she got to the kitchen, it was empty. She backtracked into the living room, and this time noticed his feet propped up on the end of the sofa. He'd fallen asleep watching TV again.

Smiling, she leaned over to wake him and immediately smelled the liquor on his breath, then saw the empty bottle on the floor beside him. Her heart dropped. Not again. He'd been down in the dumps ever since he'd stopped going out with Flynn's mom, Mona, and this was always his cure-all when things didn't go as planned. It used to scare her, finding him in this condition, but not any longer. She'd made up her mind months ago that they weren't quitting and moving ever again, no matter how many jobs he got fired from. She yanked the pillow out from under his head, and the remote out of his hands.

"Uncle Pat. Wake up. You're going to be late for work."

Pat Carmichael groaned then blinked as the television went dead.

"Huh . . . what . . . I uh . . ."

"Wake up! You're going to be late for work," she said, and took the empty bottle into the kitchen and dumped it into the trash.

She was making coffee when he stumbled into the kitchen.

"Hey, honey, this rain is really coming down and I'm not feeling so good. I think I'll call in sick and you can take the car to school, okay?"

Tara's heart sank. "No, Uncle Pat, it's not okay. I'm not

taking the car, because you've got thirty-three minutes to be out of his house or you're gonna be late for work."

Pat frowned. Tara had never challenged him like this before.

"Listen here, you don't—"

Tara's hands began to shake. "No, you listen. If you lose this job and decide you're going to quit on this city and move again, you'll be leaving without me. I'm done, Uncle Pat. I have less than a year to graduate high school and I'm never changing schools again. Thanks to the reward money I got for finding Bethany Fanning when she got kidnapped, I have money to go to college and I'm staying here to do it. Are you going to stay with me, or am I going to be part of the past you're still trying to outrun?"

Pat was blindsided, and at the same time, ashamed. He put his arms around his niece and hugged her.

"I will never leave you behind, and I'm sorry I scared you," he said, and kissed the top of her head. "I'm going to clean up. Make the coffee strong."

Tara blinked back tears as she poured the water into the coffee maker and turned it on.

That's been a long time coming, but I'm proud of you.

Tara sighed. The whisper in her ear was from the only motherly figure she'd ever known. Millicent was a spirit who never bothered to show herself beyond a puff of pink smoke, but she was always Tara's backup.

Henry popped in beside Tara and gave her a ghostly hug before ricocheting off the ceiling and rattling the back door, just to let her know he thought she rocked the house.

It was enough to lighten Tara's mood, and by the time she finished her cereal, Pat was downing his second cup of coffee and heading out the door with a peanut butter and jelly sandwich to eat on the way to work.

"Have a good day honey, and I love you."

"You, too, Uncle Pat and I love you, too."

Just like that, the fuss was over. Tara was about to get dressed for school when the phone rang.

"Hello?"

"Hey, girlfriend, wanna ride to school today or are you breaking out the ark?"

Tara laughed. BFFs were the best, especially BFFs like Nikki Scott. "You are too funny, and I would love a ride to school."

"I'll be there in fifteen minutes."

"Fifteen? Yikes."

Nikki laughed. "Sorry. I have to drop my sisters off at the gym for early basketball practice, so it's now or never."

"Now, and I promise I won't keep you waiting."

"Great. See you in a few," Nikki said.

Tara hung up, rinsed her cereal bowl and left it in the sink as she ran to get dressed. Ten minutes later she was standing in front of the bathroom mirror, eyeing her jeans and her orange Oklahoma State University sweatshirt. She smiled at her reflection. OSU rocked.

Because of the weather, she pulled her hair back in a ponytail, which then left her with nothing to hide behind. That used to be a big deal, but not so much anymore. The older Tara got, the more comfortable she was in her own skin. Still, if she squinted just a little and turned her head to the left, she thought she looked a little bit like Angelina Jolie, who was her all-time favorite movie star. But not because Angelina was beautiful—because she adopted children no one else wanted.

A quick slash of lip gloss and she was good to go. When Nikki drove up a couple of minutes later, Tara was standing on the porch with her raincoat on, the hood pulled up over her head, and her book bag on her shoulder.

Kiss kiss.

Tara stifled a grin. Millicent was definitely in mother mode this morning, giving her a kiss goodbye.

"As if you ever stay behind," Tara muttered, and made a mad dash into the downpour to Nikki's SUV. "OMG . . . the rain is cold," she said, as she quickly shut the door behind her.

Nikki's two younger sisters were in the back seat, giving her the once-over. They knew from Nikki that Tara was psychic and were suitably impressed.

"Hi Tara," they said in unison.

Tara glanced over her shoulder and smiled at them as Nikki drove off. They looked like different versions of Nikki, all with long dark hair, almond shaped eyes, and that beautiful skin, compliments of a mother who was part Native American.

"Hi, you guys. So you have early practice, hunh?"

Rachelle nodded and Morgan rolled her eyes.

Tara laughed. "Better you than me. I can't walk and chew gum at the same time, let alone dribble a ball and run."

"I wish I was as tall as you and Rachelle are," Morgan said. "I'd be the star on the team."

"You guys aren't through growing. Give it some time," Tara said.

Morgan rolled her eyes. "I'm not holding my breath. Look at Nikki. She's the oldest and she barely made it past five feet."

Nikki frowned. Her height was a sore spot with her, especially because her younger sister, Rachelle, was already five feet, nine inches tall and still growing. "I'm almost five feet, four inches, thank you very much."

"Which means you're only five feet, three inches," Rachelle said, and then giggled.

Tara couldn't stop smiling. She didn't have siblings, and this family banter was endearing to her, although she could tell from the look on Nikki's face that she wasn't nearly as impressed with her sisterly duties.

After they dropped the girls off at the gym, they headed back across town to Stillwater High, talking about boys and school as they went.

"So, are you and Flynn getting serious?" Nikki asked.

Tara shrugged. "I don't know. We don't talk about serious. We're just having a good time together."

Nikki nodded. "That's smart. We've got our whole lives ahead of us, right?"

Tara thought about college. "You said you were going to OSU. What are you going to study?"

"Haven't decided yet, have you?"

In my last life, I never learned to read.

Tara blinked. She should have known Millicent wouldn't stay absent for long, especially when they were talking about boys. Millicent did love the opposite sex.

"No, not yet," Tara said.

You could read palms. You'd be good at that.

Tara stifled a snort, which Millicent detected.

It was only a suggestion. Oh look! Hunk alert at three o'clock! Oops! He's in trouble.

Tara glanced out the window and to her horror saw some stranger had Flynn backed against the wall of a building. From the looks on their faces, they were close to coming to blows. Within seconds, she was nauseous from the dark energy and knew this was connected to the trouble she'd been sensing.

"Nikki. There's Flynn. Pull over, quick."

Nikki turned off the street into the parking lot of the quick stop, as horrified as Tara had been by what was happening to Flynn.

"What do we do?" Nikki asked.

"Honk the horn!" Tara said.

Nikki gave the horn three sharp blasts.

The stranger turned, obviously startled by their arrival and darted off into the alley between the buildings.

Nikki honked again and motioned for him to get in.

Flynn didn't hesitate as he ran through the rain and got into the back seat the Scott sisters had just vacated.

The darkness came with Flynn, leaving Tara struggling not to throw up her cereal as Nikki took off out of the parking lot.

"What was that all about?" Tara asked.

The hood of the poncho Flynn was wearing had slipped off when he ran, soaking his face and hair to the point that he appeared to be crying. He swiped angrily at his face and ignored her question.

It has something to do with his father, and oh my, he smells good. I remember men's cologne. Once upon a time I—

Tara frowned. *Oh for Pete's sake, Millicent. Not now.*

She heard a huff and then a pop. She'd ticked Millicent off, but that didn't mean she wouldn't be back. However, this thing with Flynn and the bad guy at the station was beginning to make sense. Flynn's father had cancer and was dying—but he was also in prison. Was the bad stuff she'd been sensing for so long actually connected to Flynn, or to his father . . . or maybe both?

She twisted in the seat until she was facing Flynn, only to find he wouldn't look at her.

"Are you alright?" she asked.

His hands were knotted into fists. "I'm fine," he muttered. "Thanks for the ride. The rain sucks."

Tara, being Tara, persisted. "Who was that man? Was he trying to rob you or something?"

"Let it go, Moon Girl. It has nothing to do with you."

And just like that, Tara's feelings were hurt. She glanced at Nikki, who shrugged and made a sad face in sympathy for the way Flynn had dissed her.

They were silent the rest of the way to school. No sooner had Nikki parked than Flynn was out of the car.

"Thanks again for the ride. See you later," he mumbled, and made a run for the door without waiting to walk Tara in like he usually did.

Tara's heart hurt, but the really awful part was that the moment Flynn left the car, the sick feeling went with him. OMG. Was it possible for a girl to become allergic to her boyfriend?

"Maybe it embarrassed or just scared him and he didn't know what to say," Nikki said.

Tara shrugged. Her feelings were hurt and she wanted to cry, but not in front of Nikki. "Maybe, but you were a sweetheart to stop like that and pick him up. I didn't think that I might be involving you in something bad."

Nikki threw a hand up in the air, as if dismissing the incident. "Pfft, I gave two of my friends a ride to school this morning. Nothing bad about that."

Tara sighed. "Well, it was a lot to me, and I really appreciate it."

Nikki smiled. "I'll see you at lunch. In the meantime, don't let the enemy see you sweat."

Tara laughed. Nikki Scott was good for her soul.

"You got it, girlfriend."

Nikki high-fived her. "Now that's what I'm talking about. Are you ready? You do know we're gonna get wet no matter how fast we move."

"LET'S DO THIS!" they squealed, opened their doors in unison, leaped into the downpour, slammed the doors behind them and headed across the parking lot to Stillwater High on the run.

They were still laughing when they ran through the front door. Coach Jones was on hall duty. Tara liked Coach Jones. He was one of the really cool teachers here.

"Good morning, ladies," he said, as they shifted from run to walk.

"Good morning, Coach," they echoed, dripping water as they made a beeline to their lockers.

"So, see you at lunch?" Nikki said.

Tara nodded. They parted company, each heading to first hour with a load of books and an acceptance that they wouldn't be free of this place for the next eight hours.

The hall was full of kids just as wet as she was, most of which were talking at a Wi-Fi pace. The hall sounded like it was full of clucking chickens. She kept looking for Flynn as she walked, but didn't see him anywhere. Okay, so he would certainly have been frightened by what had happened, but his reaction to her concern made no sense. What kind of a girlfriend would she have been if she'd ignored the whole thing?

It's about money and his father.

Tara jumped. *For real?*

For real. His father hid something . . . money I think, that also belongs to that man and his friends. They all found out he's dying, which means he won't be getting out to give up the location. The hunk is in big trouble. They're going to try to get to the father through the son.

What do I do?

YOU do nothing. You tell Flynn to tell the coppers.

Tara rolled her eyes. *It's cops, not coppers.*

She heard a pop, which meant Millicent was gone, but it was no big deal because she'd reached her classroom. Thanks to Millicent, at least now Tara knew what was wrong. She just didn't yet know what to do about it.

As usual, there was a rush to get into the room before the last bell rang. The floors were slick from the water dripping off clothes and shoes and she was hurrying. One minute she was upright and the next thing she knew her feet were in the air. This was definitely going to hurt.

Only she never hit the floor. Just as she began to fall, she felt hands beneath her elbows and suddenly she was back on her feet.

"Oh my gosh," Tara said as she turned to thank her rescuer, but all she saw was the back of a very tall guy in a long black poncho walking away. "Hey!" she yelled.

He paused and looked back.

Tara wasn't one to ever judge someone's appearance, but this guy left her speechless. He was dressed all in black, from his shirt to his shoes. His eyes were dark, his hair was black and wet, slicked back away from his face, which revealed a bad-ass widow's peak. He had a long scar on his cheek that ran down the side of his neck, with a single silver skull earring dangling from one ear. He had such a defiant expression on his face, as if he was expecting rejection, and that she immediately empathized, remembering her first day here.

"Thank you," she said, and ducked into her room just as Mrs. Farmer was closing the door.

"I saw you falling," Mrs. Farmer said. "Are you alright?"

"Yes, ma'am. Some knight in shining armor dressed a little like Dracula caught me before I hit the deck. I've never seen him before, and he's someone who'd be hard to miss."

"Oh, I believe his name is French Langdon. I think he's a transfer student. Now please take your seat. You can thank him later."

"Yes, ma'am," Tara said, and headed for her desk.

He has secrets.

Tara frowned. Millicent's info was usually helpful, but this was way off course. What kind of secrets?

The kinds of secrets that are secret.

Seriously, Millicent? Is this the best you can do?

Your teacher has twelve siblings. All boys. Her mother went mad. I see her now and then, but since that incarnation she's never been the same.

Tara blinked. She had not thought about spirits visiting each other or forming friendships, and she'd never thought about Mrs. Farmer as a kid, let alone having twelve brothers. It was an interesting concept, and she hoped when she got to the other side someday she'd get to see her mother and father. Even if she didn't remember them, it would be cool to see them again.

She forgot about French Langdon when Mrs. Farmer pulled out her text book and told them to turn to page 107. After that, she was too busy taking notes to think about the neo-Dracula of Stillwater High.

It was noon before she saw Flynn again. He was on his way out of the cafeteria as she was going in. He gave her a fake smile that didn't reach his eyes and pretended to tweak her nose, which he knew she hated.

"Hey, Tara, sorry I missed you for lunch, but I have an appointment with the counselor to make sure I'll have enough credits to graduate. The last thing I want is you leaving me behind. "

"We need to talk," Tara whispered.

Flynn frowned. "Yeah, sure, catch you later, okay?"

"Uh, yeah sure . . . later," she said, and headed for the line.

That was weird.

Tara shared Millicent's opinion. *Seriously weird.*

You know he's just sleeting you.

What? What on earth are you talking about?

You know . . . when someone is trying to put something over on another person. I believe you people call it sleeting.

Tara laughed out loud, which drew a few stares considering she was standing by herself at the back of the lunch line.

It's not sleeting, it's snowing. The phrase you're referring to is 'you're being snowed' which kind of means they're feeding you a line to cover up the truth. And just for the record, that phrase is almost as old as Uncle Pat.

Ah. I knew it had something to do with the weather. What's for lunch? Oooh, oooh, strawberries! I love strawberries. There was this Duke I knew. Once after a masked ball he ate strawberries off my bare—

Stop! Stop! Telling me that is wrong on so many levels!

Whatever. About those strawberries, are you—

I'm getting strawberries, okay, and every time I take a big, juicy bite I'll think of you, how's that?

It will suffice.

A serving of salad, a plate of macaroni and cheese and a bowl of berries later, Tara was carrying her tray toward the table where Nikki and her BFFs, Mac and Penny, were sitting.

They saw her coming and waved.

She couldn't help thinking what a change this was from her first week at school. Being the new girl during the senior year of high school had been the worst, but it was getting better. Lots of people still thought she was weird, but the only student here at school who continued to give her a hard time was Prissy Marshall. Like it was Tara's fault Prissy cheated on a test and got kicked off the cheerleading squad. All Tara had done was give her a heads up that she'd been found out. The rest of that karma was all on Prissy.

"Flynn just left," Nikki said, as Tara slid into a seat beside her.

"We talked. He's on his way to the counselor's office to check on some of his credits."

Nikki dunked a French fry in ketchup then popped it in her mouth. "So he's okay, then?"

Tara shrugged. "No, he's not okay, but he wants me to think so. I think it's complicated, so unless he offers to share his misery, I'll pretend I don't know a thing about it."

Nikki laughed. "Is he dense or what? Like . . . did he suddenly forget that you 'know' stuff?"

Tara grinned. "He's a guy. We have to cut them some slack, right?"

Mac and Penny thought that was hilarious and added their

laughter to the table.

"And speaking of guys, did you all see the new one? He has a scar on his face that looks like a snake. He is seriously bad-ass," Penny said.

Nikki gasped. "For real? Ooh, imagine waking up every day with a guy like that beside you."

The four of them looked at each other and then giggled in unison. From all appearances, four carefree teens were just having lunch in the high school cafeteria.

The lunch hour had passed, and then so did the rest of the day. Tara was pretty ticked. Flynn managed to dodge her all day, and by the time school was out, he had already made his getaway. The only good thing about the entire day was that it had finally stopped raining.

After Nikki dropped Tara off at home, it was business as usual. She started homework along with supper, and by the time Uncle Pat got off work, she had beans and wieners coming out of the oven and a skillet of fried potatoes ready and waiting.

"Something smells good," Pat said, as he set his lunch box on the cabinet. "Ooh, beans and wieners. We haven't had that in ages. Give me a couple of minutes to get out of these wet clothes and I'll help you set the table."

"I'll do it, Uncle Pat. You need to take a hot shower before supper. You don't want to get sick."

"Good idea," he said. "I'll hurry."

Tara sat back down at the kitchen table to her homework, popped the ear buds back into her ears and conjugated Spanish verbs to Adele's 'Rollin' in the Deep'. The song fit her mood. She felt sad and off-center. Being on the outs with your boyfriend made days like that happen.

All of a sudden, Henry popped up in front of her, looking anxious and waving his hands. At that moment, there was a knock at the door, but Tara didn't hear it because of the music. Henry knocked over the salt shaker to increase his insistence.

She looked up and frowned. "What?"

Henry pointed. Tara took the ear buds out of her ears just as another knock sounded.

"Oh. Someone's at the door. Thank you, Henry. You are such a doll," Tara said, and blew him a kiss.

It discombobulated Henry to the point that he dissipated in pieces. First his feet—then his arms—then the rest of his body. His head was the last to disappear, but he was smiling as he went.

Tara was still grinning when she got to the door, and then was surprised to see two detectives from the Stillwater police department. She'd helped Detectives Allen and Rutherford solve two crimes already and thought of them as friends, only neither one was smiling.

"Hi guys," Tara said.

"Miss Luna. We need to ask you some questions. Is your uncle here?"

Tara frowned. "Miss Luna? What happened to Tara? Did I jaywalk somewhere?"

Detective Rutherford shrugged. "This is serious business, Tara. Can we come in?"

She grinned. "That's way better, and sure, you can come in. Uncle Pat is taking a shower. It was a nasty day for reading meters. I'll tell him you're here. In the meantime, have a seat."

Detective Allen frowned as Tara walked away. "Dang it, Rutherford. Police business is no joke."

Rutherford frowned. "Do you see me laughing?"

"No, but you're being too friendly with a person of interest."

"She's not a person of interest. Freak of nature, maybe. Interesting doesn't even being to describe it."

Allen frowned back. Before they could get into an argument of their own, Tara was back with her uncle at her heels. He was pulling a t-shirt over his head and his feet were bare as he entered the living room.

"What's going on?" Pat asked.

"We just need to ask Tara some questions," Detective Allen said. "If you both wouldn't mind having a seat, we'll get out of your way as soon as possible."

Pat sat, then looked at Tara. "What did you do?"

Before Tara could answer, the magazine on the table beside

Pat's elbow flew up into the air and landed with a splat in his lap.

Both detectives were on their feet.

"What the hell?" Pat yelped.

Tara eyes narrowed. "Obviously, your assumption that I would automatically be at fault ticked Millicent off, and it set my teeth a bit on edge, as well. Why would you instantly think I'd done something wrong?"

Rutherford was standing by the door. Allen was up against the wall. They'd already had more than one run-in with her ghosts and didn't want a repeat performance.

"We can talk from here," Rutherford said.

"Talk about what?" Tara asked.

"We're investigating a homicide," Allen said.

Tara leaned forward with her elbows on her knees. "So, do you need my help or something? I don't mind—"

"I do," Pat said.

"No, it's not that, exactly," Rutherford said. "We have a body. We have identified the man. We also have surveillance tape of that man inside a convenience store earlier this morning, then the clerk's account that he accosted someone outside a few minutes after his arrival."

Tara's stomach turned. She knew before he opened his mouth again what he was going to say.

"And," Rutherford continued. "In the background of that tape, you are sitting in a gray SUV, watching it happen. We would like your version of this account, and for you to confirm the identity of the person who the clerk identified, also running toward your car and getting inside."

Pat gasped.

Tara sighed.

If you need to make a getaway, I can distract them.

"No, Millicent, I am not making a getaway. Chill, okay?"

The lights went on and off a couple of times, which was enough to set the detectives teeth on edge. Tara was afraid that one more stunt from Millicent and they would finish this interview at police headquarters, which was the last place she wanted to be.

"Of course I know who it was," Tara said. "My friend was giving me a ride to school so I wouldn't have to walk in the rain. We were passing this convenience store when I saw my boyfriend, Flynn, talking to some man outside. You remember Flynn O'Mara. He helped rescue Bethany Fanning, the cheerleader who was kidnapped. We pulled in to give him a ride, too, and when we honked, the man he was talking to saw us and ran off down an alley. Flynn got in and we went to school."

It was a simpler reason than they'd expected and certainly took some of the wind from their sails. Rutherford was writing as he talked. "So, did Flynn say who the man was or what they were talking about?"

"No sir."

"He didn't say a word?"

Tara sighed. "No. I could tell he was bothered about it, but he tried to pretend he wasn't. I'm not hiding anything, but I know more about this than Flynn thinks I do."

Allen took a step forward. "Exactly how do you know—"

Rutherford elbowed him. "Remember who you're talking to."

"Oh. Yeah. So, what do you know?" Allen asked.

"I know what Millicent told me."

Rutherford ran a finger around his shirt collar, as if it had suddenly gotten too tight. This was where writing up a report on their interview with Tara Luna was going to make them look like a pair of dumb asses.

"You *are* referring to your ghost and not a living breathing person who you know?" Rutherford asked, then looked nervous and added. "Uh . . . meaning no disrespect or anything, but exactly what do you call someone like her?"

Tara was getting angry, and a little bit hurt. She thought they'd already cleared the air between them with this stuff.

"I call her Millicent. Now, do you care what I know, or are we going around the mulberry bush again and pretend you're surprised by all this? You both know I see ghosts. We dug up a decades old murder victim out of our backyard so you both know I'm psychic. How many times do I have to prove it before you all get over it?"

"Well, damn it . . . excuse my language," Rutherford said. "We didn't mean to hurt your feelings, but it was a surprise to see you in that tape."

"It is a bigger surprise to me that the man I saw this morning is now dead. You both need to sit down so you can write your notes."

They went back to their chairs.

Pat slid a hand across her shoulder. "Are you in any danger, honey?"

"No, of course not, Uncle Pat. We just picked up Flynn and took him to school." Then she turned her attention to the cops. "Are you ready?"

They nodded.

"So, here's the scoop, and FYI, Flynn does not know I know this, because we haven't talked about it, and he doesn't want to be around me, so I'm guessing he thinks if he keeps his distance, I won't know. But I digress. According to Millicent, the man who pushed Flynn up against the wall isn't actually interested in Flynn, other than his connection to someone else. It's about his father, Michael O'Mara."

Detective Allen frowned. "But he's in prison."

Tara nodded. "And that's the problem. It has to do with money. Before Michael O Mara went to prison, he was with a gang of bad guys. He hid a bunch of their money and then got sent to prison. The men were waiting for him to get out so they could split it up, I guess. At any rate, they don't know where it is and now they are running out of time."

Rutherford had quit writing and was just staring at Tara in disbelief.

She paused. "What?"

He shook his head. "I'm hearing this come out of your mouth, and I still can't believe it. You just 'know' stuff that would take us weeks, maybe months to find out, if even then. I'm sorry, I interrupted. So they don't know where the money is? What's the big hurry all of a sudden to find out? I mean, O'Mara's been in the pen for almost three years now."

"Because Michael O'Mara is dying of cancer and they probably found out. Now the men are going to try to get to the father through the son before it's too late."

"Did you see Flynn at school during the day?"

Tara frowned. "We all went inside at the same time this morning. I saw him at noon on his way to the counselor's office to discuss some school credit issue, and I did not see him after school, which isn't unusual on nights he buses tables at Eskimo Joe's. Why don't you talk to him?"

"Because he's gone missing. His mother is in a panic. Claims she has no idea where he's at, and we have a dead man on our hands with a connection to Flynn."

Tara jumped to her feet. She was starting to panic, too. He shouldn't be missing. This wasn't good. "What time of day was the man murdered?"

"The M.E. says before noon."

Tara frowned. "And did you talk to Flynn's teachers to see if he was in all his classes?"

Detective Allen fidgeted with the pen he was holding. "According to the teachers, he answered roll in every class and didn't ask to be excused in any of them."

Tara gasped, and when she did, the lights started going on and off in the room and pages started flying out of Detective Allen's notebook. He was too scared to move. She was so angry her voice was shaking.

"I can't believe you just did this. You knew all along that Flynn had nothing to do with that man's murder, and yet everything you said to me earlier was deceptive. You let me talk, then you led me to believe Flynn could be responsible for this dead man and were viewing him as a suspect, when all along you knew he was missing!"

"It's called interviewing a witness to a crime," Allen said.

"Well then, you're both sitting in the wrong house, because I did not witness a crime today, and you both know Flynn didn't either. Are you looking for Flynn? Is there a missing person's report out?"

"Well—"

Tara stomped to the door and yanked it open. All the papers that had been flying around the room went shooting out the door. "If I find out anything else that will be of benefit to your case, I will call you."

Pat stood up. He was as aggravated at them as Tara was, but knew it was wise to err on the side of courtesy.

"Gentlemen, if you're done, our supper's getting cold."

Since Detective Allen had already booked it out the door, Detective Rutherford was trying to maintain his composure. "Right. So, if you hear from Flynn, you'll let us know?"

Tara's voice was shaking. "I just told you that people are trying to force Michael O'Mara to give up the hiding place of a bunch of money and use Flynn to do it. Now he's missing, and you think he's hiding out? You don't know Flynn. He would never run off and leave his mother at the mercy of these people. If he's missing, he's in trouble. He needs your help."

Tara burst into tears and ran out of the room.

Rutherford paused at the threshold. "I like your niece, okay? Tell her we're sorry we upset her."

"I like her, too, and she's right. You both knew coming in here that the boy wasn't a suspect, and yet you let her think it, trying to trick her into saying something that would incriminate one or both of them. If someone has snatched Mona's son, then find the boy and you'll find your murderer. I think we're done here."

He closed the door in their faces.

Rutherford looked at his partner, who was out in the yard picking up the papers from his notebook, then shook his head and headed for the car.

Inside, Pat went to Tara's room and found her face down on her bed, sobbing.

Chapter Two

"Tara, sweetheart . . ."

Tara sat up and threw her arms around her uncle Pat's neck. "I'm scared, Uncle Pat. Something has happened to Flynn that isn't good, I can feel it."

Pat was sick, thinking of how frightened Mona must be. "Do you want to go over to his house after we eat?"

"Yes, oh yes, Uncle Pat. Maybe if I'm there I can pick up on something that might help find him."

Pat gave her a hug. "That's my girl. Thinking positive is always the best. Now go wash your face and let's eat. I'm starved, and the food smells so good I can't wait to dig in."

Relieved that they had a plan, Tara washed the tears from her face and followed her uncle into the kitchen. He was already putting food on the table and making their drinks.

"Do you want iced tea?"

She nodded and started to help, but he shooed her toward the table.

"I got this. You cooked. After we eat, I'll clean up and then we'll head over to Mona's."

Tara ate without tasting the food, anxious to get out of the house. She kept sending mental signals to Millicent and Henry, but they'd made themselves suspiciously absent, which usually meant they knew answers to what she would ask, but weren't allowed to tell her.

The lights were off when Pat and Tara arrived at the O'Mara residence. Pat frowned. "Looks like she's gone."

Tara closed her eyes and focused. In her mind, she could see Flynn's mother sitting in a chair in the dark. She looked terrified.

"No, she's there, and she's really scared, Uncle Pat."

"That settles it," he said. "We're going in, no matter what. Come on."

The moment they got up the steps Pat knocked loudly. "Mona, it's me, Pat. Tara is with me. Let us in."

Within seconds, the door swung inward. She took one look at them and then burst into tears. Pat hugged her as Tara locked the door and then followed them into the living room. Mona sat down between them and grabbed their hands.

"The police were here. They said Flynn had an argument with a man this morning and now the man is dead. He didn't come home from school and he hasn't called," Mona whispered. "If he's going to be late, he always calls. What's happening?"

Pat frowned. "What did the police say to you?"

Mona started crying. "They want to talk to Flynn about the murder. Flynn wouldn't kill anyone. I don't understand why this is happening."

Tara was furious. The police had been as deceptive with Mona as they had with them. "The police already know Flynn didn't kill that man. They're just trying to trick us into saying something incriminating."

Mona blinked. "Us, trick us? Are you involved?"

Tara felt Mona's emotions shift to a need to blame her for what was happening, but she couldn't be farther from the truth.

"Only to the extent of seeing some man pin Flynn against the wall of a convenience store this morning. Because of the rain, Nikki Scott was giving me a ride to school. We saw Flynn and stopped to pick him up, too. When we honked to get his attention, the man who was talking to him ran away. We gave Flynn a ride, but he wouldn't talk to me about anything."

Mona moaned.

Pat squeezed her hand. "There's more, Mona, and you're going to have to be strong."

Mona looked at Tara in horror. "You know something? Oh my God, is he dead? Is Flynn dead?"

Tara didn't know how to answer without making it worse.

"I haven't been able to get a connection to him, but I know something about why the man was bothering Flynn. I'm sorry, but it has to do with Flynn's father."

Mona groaned. "What is it? Tell me."

"There are some men who were associated with your ex-husband. He hid a bunch of their money, then got arrested and sent to prison. They don't know where he hid it, and were willing to wait until he got out, but then they somehow found out about the cancer. They are afraid he'll die without revealing the location and they're trying to get to Michael through Flynn."

Mona's panic turned quickly to anger. "Even in prison he's still ruining our lives."

Pat took her hand. "Mona, listen to me. I've been thinking about this ever since Tara told us what was going on. I don't know where Flynn is, but I'd lay big odds that they're taking good care of him. If they want Michael's cooperation, they will have to assure him that Flynn has come to no harm."

She shivered. "Yes, yes, that makes sense. I pray that you're right, because if anything ever happened to Flynn, I would die. He's all I have."

Mona's despair was swamping Tara's ability to focus. She needed to put some distance between them if she had a chance of making a connection with Flynn.

"Uh, Mrs. O'Mara, you know a little bit about how things work with me, right?"

"I guess so, but why?"

"May I go into Flynn's room? Maybe if I touch some of his things I can get a connection with him."

"Down the hall, last door on your left. Go, go, do whatever you do. Find my boy, Tara. Please."

"I can't promise anything, but I'll try."

Tara got up quickly and left her uncle and Mona talking quietly on the sofa. Tara's hands were sweating and her stomach was in knots. She had never wanted her skills to work as much as she did right now.

The moment she walked into Flynn's room she felt sad and afraid. They were his emotions, not hers, and it made her even more anxious to find his location before something else happened.

Her voice was shaking as she moved to the dresser. "Millicent. Henry. Where are you guys? Why aren't you helping me here?"

He's alive.

Tara was so relieved that she started to cry. Tears were rolling down her face as she pushed his hairbrush aside to get some tissues, and the moment she touched the brush, she was in his head, hearing his voice, feeling his pain and his fear.

These ropes are too tight. I can't feel my hands. I can't believe this is happening. I need to get word to Mom. These guys are total screw-ups and they'll come after her next. It's all Dad's fault. If he hadn't gotten mixed up with them, none of this would be happening.

Suddenly Tara was seeing the room through Flynn's eyes. It looked like a seedy motel, but there wasn't anything in sight to tell her where it was. Then she watched the door open. She felt Flynn's adrenaline surge, and when she saw the man who walked in, she understood why. The man was huge—both tall and heavy, with long gray/brown hair and a full gray beard, but she couldn't see enough of his features to be able to identify him.

"Well, boy, looks like we don't need your help after all. Your old man is dead, so we're gonna have to revamp the set-up."

"Dad's dead? No! You're lying."

Tara felt the shock and then a wave of sorrow sweep through him. She was crying with him as he struggled to get free of the ropes.

"No lie, kid. That's what our source told us, and we're none too happy about it ourselves. Bringing you here to McAlester to visit him at the prison was a waste of time."

"Does that mean you're letting me go?"

"What it means is that we're gonna have to shift focus. We found out your mama paid your daddy a visit here at the prison a few weeks back, and

we're thinkin' that if old Mike knew he was dying, he'd be tellin' someone about that money. We're thinkin' he told your mama where it is, and now she's gonna have to cough it up before we can let you go."

"No, Sam. You're wrong. Dad wouldn't do that. He'd know Mom wouldn't take it. He'd know that she'd tell the police, first."

"Sorry. I'm not buyin' that story. We're about to bet your life that you're wrong, because if your mama don't cough up that money, you'll both be joinin' your old man a lot faster than you planned."

Tara gasped, and just like that, the link was gone. But she'd seen and heard enough. Now she needed to tell the police. She ran out of his room and back up the hall.

"Uncle Pat! You need to call the police now!"

Mona jumped up and grabbed Tara's arm. "What did you see? Tell me! Is he alive?"

"Yes, ma'am, he's alive."

Mona's eyes rolled back in her head as she fainted. Pat caught her, and laid her down on the sofa. When he wanted to fuss over her, Tara grabbed him by the arm.

"Uncle Pat, hurry. Make the call," then she sat down to wait for the police to arrive.

Detective Allen was at his desk when the call came in. He paged Rutherford, who was at his son's Boy Scout meeting. It took less than fifteen minutes for them to get to the O'Mara house.

"What are you two doing here?" Rutherford asked, as Uncle Pat let them in.

Tara stood up. Her hands were shaking, but her voice was firm.

"We're here because this is the closest I could get to Flynn, and I needed a connection. He's in trouble. A big heavy-set man with long gray/brown hair and a bushy gray beard is holding Flynn hostage. Flynn called him Sam. He's in a motel in the town where the prison is located, but I don't know the name. They were going to make him visit his father tomorrow at the penitentiary and get the location of the money, only Michael

O'Mara died tonight so they're shifting focus to Mrs. O'Mara. They think because she visited him in prison a few weeks earlier that he surely told her where he hid this money."

Rutherford shoved a hand through his hair. "O'Mara died?"

Tara shrugged. "It's what Sam said."

"Allen, check that out, will you?" Rutherford asked.

His partner nodded and stepped outside to make the call as Rutherford eyed Mona.

"Mrs. O'Mara, did you visit your ex-husband recently?"

"Only once, a few weeks ago, right after I found out he had cancer. There were some hard feelings between us and I didn't want him to die without making peace."

"Yes, ma'am, but did he mention any money?"

"No, no, but I wish to God he had, because then I would have something to tell the men who have Flynn."

"You need to hide her," Tara said. "As long as they can't find her, they'll keep Flynn alive. The minute she tells them what she just told you, he's dead."

Rutherford looked nervous. "Is that what you heard this Sam guy say?"

"What he said was that if Mona didn't help, they would be joining his father."

Mona gasped.

Detective Allen came back inside. "She was right. O'Mara died this evening." He eyed Tara curiously, as if trying to figure out how her brain worked.

"It's a really run-down motel," Tara offered.

"There's one other thing," Allen said. "Our murder victim has an older brother named Sam."

Rutherford spun. "Then we might just know the name of the man who has Flynn, which means we can get a make and model on the car he drives and search motels in and around McAlester." He looked at Tara and grinned. "You really need to rethink my suggestion a few months ago and become a detective when you're out of college. We could sure use someone like you."

Tara glared. "I don't think I'd like to be a detective. I know

I didn't like being grilled and lied to this morning."

"Uh, yeah, sorry about that, but we didn't actually lie," Allen said.

Rutherford wasn't going to apologize. "We were just doing our job, and that's what we're going to do now. Mrs. O'Mara, do you have any relatives out of town . . . or someplace to go that these men wouldn't know about?"

"I'm not leaving town and I'm not leaving this house. If I'm their next target, then that may be the only way to get my son back."

Rutherford argued. "You heard Tara. You can't help him if you don't know the location of the money, but you need to find a place to hide and stay out of sight. It'll give us time to find your son."

"Then you need to start looking and find him, because I'm not budging. He's my son—my life. If I need to be the lure that brings them here, then so be it."

Tara watched her uncle put his arm around Mona and swallowed back tears. This was awful, knowing just enough to panic, but not sure it was enough to help Flynn out of this mess.

"Are you notifying the local authorities in McAlester to look for that man car?" Mona asked.

"Yes, ma'am. Detective Allen is already relaying the info to our department. They'll coordinate the search with the McAlester PD," Rutherford said. "And, if you're determined to stay here, we'll put a police unit on your street until we have the kidnappers in custody . . . if we can find them, that is."

"Do what you need to do," Pat said. "Mona won't be alone. We'll stay."

"Promise you'll call?" Tara asked.

Rutherford eyed the tears in Tara's eyes. "Yeah, kid, I promise."

Flynn's head hurt from crying.

This was, without doubt, the worst day of his life. Kidnapped right off his own front porch, then hog-tied and thrown into the floorboard of Sam

Nettles' truck. They drove for what felt like hours and then dragged him into this nasty motel room after dark and tied him up to a chair. He couldn't believe his dad was dead and he hadn't had a chance to say goodbye. He kept thinking of his mother and of Tara, wondering if he'd ever see them again.

The two guys who came with Sam were asleep on the bed. Sam had dozed off in a chair, but the gun in his lap was scary enough to keep Flynn still. He didn't want the man to wake up in a panic and shoot him by mistake.

All of a sudden he saw a shadow pass by the window outside the room, and then another shadow, and then a third. His heart started to pound.

Boom! The door flew inward, hitting the wall with a thud.

"Police! Police! Hands up! Now!"

Sam Nettles jerked as he woke. The gun he was holding slid to the floor as police slapped him and the other two men in handcuffs and hauled them out of the room so fast Flynn thought he was dreaming.

Then an officer came toward him. "Are you Flynn O'Mara?"

Flynn was too shocked to do anything but nod as the man cut the ropes from his wrists and ankles. His arms were so numb he could barely move them.

"Are you all right? Did they hurt you?"

"No sir," Flynn said. "But I think they would have. Can I go home?"

"There are a couple of cops on the way from Stillwater to pick you up. Hang tough, kid. As soon as we get your story, we'll have you home before morning."

Tara sat up with a gasp and looked around the room in confusion. Where was she? OMG, they were still at Flynn's house, and after that dream she'd just had, she was about as certain as a teenage psychic could be that the McAlester police had just rescued Flynn from the motel. Still, Rutherford had promised that he'd call if it happened, and the phone wasn't ringing.

Mona had gone to her room about two hours earlier and Pat had fallen asleep in the recliner. The phone was right by the sofa where Tara was lying. She stared at it, willing it to ring. But it didn't, and the longer time passed, the more anxious she became. What if that had been nothing more than just a dream of wishful thinking?

Her heart sank.

It was 2:00 a.m. when the call came, and all Tara could do was hold her breath, waiting for Mona to answer. Pat sat up in the recliner. Tara looked at her uncle then put a hand over her mouth, too scared to speak.

All of a sudden they heard a door bang against the wall and then Mona came out of her room, crying.

Pat ran toward her. Tara stood up, but was too scared to move.

"They found him! They found him!" Mona screamed, and then collapsed in Pat's arms.

Tara sat back down because her legs would no longer hold her.

"Is he okay?" Pat asked.

"He's fine. I talked to him. The two detectives who were here have gone to get him. They said they'd be back by daybreak."

"What about the men who kidnapped him?" Pat asked.

"They're all three in custody."

"All's well that ends well," Pat said, and gave her a hug. "It's a little early for breakfast, but none of us are going to be able to go back to sleep. I'll make coffee."

"I have some sweet rolls," Mona said, and then laughed because her relief was so great that it was either that or cry all over again.

It isn't over.

Tara's heart sank. She already knew that, but hearing Millicent say it only made the fear worse. She crawled back onto the sofa, laid down and pulled the afghan back up over her shoulders.

Hiding won't make it go away.

I know that. Who killed the man who was talking to Flynn? Surely not that Sam guy . . . he wouldn't kill his own brother, would he?"

Silence.

Tara frowned and then whispered, "Millicent? Henry?"

To her disgust, they had made themselves absent. She never

understood why they popped up in her life at the most inopportune times, and then when she really needed a question answered, they got all vague and disappeared.

Her stomach hurt and so did her head. She wanted to cry, but it would solve nothing but make her uncle Pat realize she knew something they didn't. Something hard was under her elbow. She shifted enough to realize she'd been lying on her cell phone and picked it up to check for messages. There was one from Nikki, but it was over a couple of hours old.

Do you and Flynn want to go get Hideaway pizza tomorrow night with Corey and me?

She swallowed past the lump in her throat. If only her life was as simple as Nikki's. Why did she have to be born so weird? She couldn't imagine how cool it would be to just live your life without seeing ghosts and bad things happening to people.

But then you wouldn't know us.

All of a sudden you're back? Then Tara sighed. "I know, Millicent, and I love you both. I don't want you out of my life. I just wish life was a little less chaotic sometimes, that's all."

Henry popped up with a sad look on his face and began blowing her kisses. She sighed again, and managed a half-hearted smile.

"Okay, okay, I'm over the pity party. But you guys have to do more than blow kisses and tell me how to behave. If I need you—really need you—you have to come through for me, as well. Deal?"

Deal.

Henry high-fived her as a pink puff of smoke slid across her line of vision.

"Hey, Tara, Mona made you some hot chocolate and she has honey buns . . . your favorite."

"I'll be right there," Tara said.

She wasn't sure if she could swallow without bursting into tears, but she had to give it her best try. Mona and Uncle Pat didn't need more worries tonight, and she didn't have anything helpful to tell them.

It was 6:45 a.m. when they heard a car pull up into the driveway.

Mona ran to the window. "They're here, and there's Flynn! Oh thank the lord!" She ran out onto the porch to meet him.

Uncle Pat was in the kitchen doing dishes. Tara began folding up the afghan and looking for her purse. She had something to say to Flynn and then she was going to school.

Flynn came inside talking, but the moment he saw Tara in his living room, he stopped. "Uh, I didn't know you'd be—"

Still smarting from being shut out, Tara put her hands on her hips. "We're just leaving, but FYI . . . you are a dumb ass."

Mona frowned.

"Hey," Flynn muttered. "I got kidnapped, my dad just died, and that's how you're gonna play it?"

"No, Flynn. I don't *play* at all when something this bad happens, and I'm so very sorry that your father died. But you have me to thank for the fact you're even standing in this house, and it is *no* thanks to you. I thought you trusted me. Obviously, you don't. But you need to remember that, like it or not, when something goes wrong with the people I care about, it is in their best interests to accept that I am going to know and probably interfere. I have this thing that I do, called being psychic? Remember?"

"Tara, ease up," Pat said.

"Oh, I'm easy all over the place," Tara said. "Are the cops still here?"

Flynn felt guilty and sad and mad all at the same time. He knew she was right, but so was he. This was his mess and it was dangerous. He'd lied to her for a reason, or so he'd thought—to keep her safe.

"They're outside," he said.

She glanced up at her uncle. "I'll be outside when you're ready to leave." She headed for the door with her head up and tears in her eyes.

"Tara, wait," Flynn said. "I didn't tell you because I knew how dangerous they were. I didn't want you involved."

She paused. "Yeah, I get that, but I don't know how to turn

off who I am, and you should know that, too. If I was a doctor and you were bleeding, you would have willingly come to me to fix it. I know stuff Flynn. They could have killed you and it would have been the biggest regret of my life that I knew what was happening and the cops wouldn't have been able to find you until it was too late. Yes, your dad died, but you knew it was going to happen because he was sick. How do you think your mom would have felt if you'd died tonight, too? Hunh, Flynn? How about that?"

She sailed past him, her chin trembling.

Flynn felt like he'd been sideswiped. He'd been accosted, kidnapped, learned his dad was dead, rescued by the cops, and then to come home to this was more than he could handle. He would have expected almost any kind of reaction from Tara except for her to be angry at him. His shoulders slumped as he watched her go out the door.

"She'll get over it. Really glad this turned out okay," Pat said, and patted him on the shoulder as he followed her out.

Tara was sad, but there were things left to be done. She walked across the street to where the police were parked. Rutherford was talking to the cop in the cruiser who'd been on guard.

"We need to talk," Tara said.

Rutherford glanced at Allen. They walked to the end of the car where she was standing.

"Look, you did real good helping us find him. We've got the kidnappers in custody and—"

"You have a body in the morgue and none of those men had anything to do with it. I don't know who did it, but I am telling you now that until you find the killer, Flynn and his mother are still in danger. Someone wants that money, and they're coming after her next and will use Flynn to force her to tell."

"Well shit, excuse my language," Rutherford muttered. "Are you sure?"

She glared.

Detective Allen sighed. "We hear you. We'll keep an eye on

them, but they've both refused to leave. Flynn said he's not running, and his mother said the same."

"Whatever," Tara said. "I'm going home."

Her uncle Pat was waiting for her in the car when she got in.

"Are you okay, honey?" he asked.

Tara took a deep, shaky breath. "No, but we need to hurry so I'm not late for school."

"I can write you an excuse if you want to stay home."

Tara swiped at the tears on her cheeks. "I don't want to stay home."

He squeezed her hand. "Then I'll drop you off on my way to work. I've already called in to let them know I'll be a little late. I told the boss enough about what happened to keep him from being ticked, so we're both good to go."

Tara leaned back and closed her eyes as Pat drove away. Her heart hurt. Her feelings were hurt. She was scared for Flynn and his mom, and she was scared even more that she wouldn't find out who was behind this until it was too late.

Chapter Three

Tara was numb by the time she got to school. She was tired and side-tracked, still worrying about Flynn, but hurt and angry at the same time. The last bell had already rung by the time she walked into the building so she headed straight to the office.

The principal, Mrs. Crabtree, was in the outer office. She frowned when Tara walked in. "You're late, Tara."

"Yes, ma'am." She handed the secretary her written excuse, but Mrs. Crabtree took it instead and quickly read it.

"It says here there was an emergency, but it doesn't say what kind."

Tara sighed. "It was personal, Mrs. Crabtree. My uncle signed the note."

The office door opened behind Tara. Mrs. Crabtree's eyes widened, and then she said "AHA!" in such a loud voice that Tara jumped as Mrs. Crabtree pointed.

"You think this flimsy excuse is going to get past me? You two are a couple and you're both late for school. Let me see *your* note, young man." and snatched the note right out of Flynn's hand.

Flynn looked at Tara and shrugged as he handed it over.

Only Mrs. Crabtree's indignation ended as swiftly as it had come.

"Uh . . . er . . . uh . . . this note is from the Stillwater Police Department."

"Yes, ma'am," Flynn said. "I had to finish giving my statement this morning."

Mrs. Crabtree frowned. "Statement? Were you arrested?"

"No, ma'am. I was kidnapped yesterday afternoon. The police found me and rescued me in McAlester this morning around 2:00 a.m. I wouldn't be here at all today except that we're having a big test in Spanish that I didn't want to make up."

Mrs. Crabtree gasped. "You were kidnapped?"

"Yes, ma'am. It had to do with some stuff my dad had been mixed up in. The police found me only because Tara was helping them, or I'd still be tied to a chair in that motel."

Tara's heart skipped a beat. She hadn't expected him to acknowledge that, not that she needed a pat on the back or anything.

Mrs. Crabtree saw the rope burns on his wrists and the dark circles under his eyes. "Are you alright? Should you be here, I mean?"

"There's a police car waiting for me out in the parking lot. I need to take that test, and then they're taking me home to be with my Mom. I'll be gone from school for the next two days for my father's funeral."

"Your father died?"

"Yes, ma'am."

Now the principal's frown was completely gone. "I'm very sorry for your loss."

"Thank you."

The principal kept looking from Tara to Flynn and back again. She was about to ask another question when the door suddenly opened and then slammed shut behind them again, only there was no one there.

Tara blinked. That would be Millicent, and she was obviously ticked. She just did not like Mrs. Crabtree.

Mrs. Crabtree was very familiar with the crazy stuff that happened when Tara was around. The last time she'd confronted Tara Luna, she'd gone home with a black mustache drawn on her upper lip from a runaway permanent marker. She'd had to bleach her skin to get it off, her lip had peeled, and it had taken a week for the bleach smell under her nose to go away. She wanted no part of the girl or her spooks. She looked down at the notes. She'd never gotten one from the police department on a student's behalf before.

"Write them a hall pass," she told the school secretary, and then bolted into her office and closed the door.

Tara got her note and walked out, heading to first hour as fast as she could walk. She didn't want to talk to Flynn and then be all red-eyed and crying when she got into class. But she didn't walk fast enough and Flynn caught up with her halfway down the hall.

"Tara, wait."

She pointed to the hall monitor and kept on walking.

Flynn sighed. She was really mad, but so was he. His uncles down in Ardmore were already planning his dad's funeral. Flynn couldn't wrap his head around the fact he'd never talk to him again. He knew he should have told someone about Floy Nettles threatening him yesterday morning. It might have stopped Floy's brother, Sam, from kidnapping him, but it was too late to change what had happened. It was frightening to learn that someone killed Floy only hours after Floy had confronted him, and they still didn't know who had done it.

He watched Tara walking away, and could tell by the stiff set of shoulders and her long, hurried stride that he'd hurt her feelings by shutting her out. He was so used to taking care of business on his own that it had never occurred to him to dump his troubles on anyone. However, knowing what she could do, as she'd said, he *had* been something of a dumb ass not to ask for help, and was man enough to admit it. If she'd only give him a chance to apologize, it might help unwind the knot in the pit of his belly.

Tara knew Flynn was watching her, but she kept on walking. She wanted to talk to him, too, but they couldn't do it now, and she didn't want an audience when it did happen.

He's sorry.

Tara sighed. *So am I.*

He's very sad.

I know. His father died.

Well duh.

OMG! Tara gasped. Of course Millicent knew that. In fact, Michael O'Mara and Millicent were in the same place now. If Flynn's dad would come to her, she could talk to him. She could find out where that money was hidden and turn it over to the police. Then whoever was still out there would have no reason to come after Flynn.

Millicent! You need to find—

Pop!

She caught a glimpse of pink smoke just before she heard the pop.

Well great. Millicent left without a word of goodbye and Tara was at her classroom. She had to go inside. Why did everything have to be so complicated?

Flynn left the building after he took his Spanish test. Tara saw him getting into the police car and leaving during the break between classes, but so did a lot of other students. By the next break it was all over school that Flynn O'Mara had gotten arrested. Everyone was giving Tara funny looks, as if by association alone she'd become tainted, too.

Tara hated the little gossip mill that was part of school life, but there wasn't much she could do about it. She was heading to her locker to grab a new notebook when her old nemesis, Prissy, cornered her in the hall.

"Hey, Lunatic. We saw your boyfriend getting arrested. Are you next?"

Tara glared. "Get out of my way, Prissy. You're going to make me late to class."

Prissy didn't move fast enough to suit Millicent.

All of a sudden Prissy went flying backwards, scattering books and people in her wake.

Tara grabbed a notebook out of her locker and walked away.

"Hey! She pushed me! Did you guys see that? She pushed me!" Prissy yelled.

Two of the girls from the cheerleader squad were passing by right after Prissy went down. Head cheerleader, Bethany Fanning, frowned as her friend Mel helped Prissy up. Prissy was persona-non-grata in their little clique since she'd gotten kicked off the cheerleader squad for cheating on a test. Bethany was not as sympathetic, but Mel still felt sorry for her.

"She didn't touch you, Prissy, and you know it," Mel whispered. "Stop making a scene and get up."

"Well, her crappy boyfriend *still* got arrested!" Prissy yelled.

Tara had been willing to ignore her, but that last shot was one too many. She turned around and headed back up the hall toward Prissy.

"OMG, she's coming back," Mel said.

Prissy's heart skipped a beat.

"Seriously, Pris, what's the matter with you?" Brittany said and walked off, leaving Prissy to face her fate alone.

"I've got to go," Mel said, and ran off as Tara came striding back, her long legs making short work of the distance.

Tara was so mad she was shaking. She stopped just inches from Prissy's face and jabbed a finger in her shoulder.

"Here's the deal, Prissy. It's a long sad story, but the bottom line is that the police were not arresting Flynn. They're protecting him. And, they were here to take him back to his mother's house because his father died last night. Flynn has had a very rough two days. He's sad. And he came to school to take an important test and now he's going home and won't be back until after the funeral."

Tara shifted the jab to Prissy's chest and proceeded to punctuate every sentence with a poke. "Now that you know this, I expect you to spread the truth to one and all, because if I hear even one more person say he got arrested today, I'm coming after you. Poke. It won't matter if you're not the one who said it. Poke. You're the one I'm coming after because you did more than your part to start the lie and it's up to you to spread the truth. Do you get my drift?" Poke, poke.

Prissy couldn't speak and barely had the sense to nod because Tara Luna looked like she was glowing. It had to be the sunlight coming through a window behind her, but it was a daunting sight just the same.

Tara gave Prissy her best evil eye and then stomped off, unaware that someone else was watching her every move—the same someone with a scar on his face who'd saved her from falling the day before.

It was lunch time before Tara caught up with Nikki. She had to let her know she and Flynn could not go out with her and boyfriend, Corey, Friday night.

She slid into a seat beside Mac and across the table from Nikki and Penny.

"I heard about Flynn's dad dying. Really sorry," Nikki said.

"Yeah, sorry," Mac and Penny echoed.

Tara nodded. She wasn't going to talk about the kidnapping at all. The less people who knew about it, the better, especially until the police arrested whoever it was who killed Floy Nettles.

"On another note, did you see the new guy?" Penny asked.

"You mean Dracula's spawn?" Mac asked, and then giggled.

Nikki frowned. "Guys . . . seriously?"

Penny sighed. "Okay . . . live and let live. To each his own. Whatever floats your boat. Is that apology enough?"

Nikki shrugged. "We don't make fun of people and we don't bully."

Mac shrugged. "Well, I seriously doubt *anyone* is bullying that guy. Did you see how tall he was? And all those black clothes, even a black poncho? OMG! Anyone with a Dracula fetish? Have I got a dude for you?"

Tara hid a grin by taking a bite of her burger. She was chewing and dunking a fry in ketchup when her inner self said *look up now.* So she did, straight into the forbidding gaze of French Langdon.

He was sitting at the table right in front of her, staring at her over Nikki's shoulder. She started to smile. After all, they'd already almost met, and he *had* saved her from a nasty spill, but the moment he knew he'd been caught, he stood up and walked away.

Tara frowned. That was weird, but then so was French Langdon. Whatever. She poked the fry into her mouth and tuned back into what the girls were saying.

"So, can you come?" Nikki asked.

Tara blinked. "Come where?"

"To the slumber party at my house Saturday night? It's my birthday and Mom and Dad said I could invite three girls."

Tara was so surprised she almost choked, then took a drink to clear her throat. "You're asking me to a slumber party?"

Nikki frowned. "Well, yeah. What's so surprising about that?"

Tara grinned. "I've never been to a slumber party before."

"You're kidding. Why not?"

Tara shrugged. "Never lived in one place long enough to make friends who asked."

Nikki laughed and then high-fived her. "Girl, you do have some life left to live. Do you think your uncle will let you come?"

"Yes, he won't care. OMG, this is amazing. I am so stoked," Tara said, and then dunked a fry in the ketchup and popped it in her mouth to celebrate.

"So. My house Saturday at 3:00 p.m. No presents. The party is my present, okay?" Nikki said.

"Deal," the girls said.

"Deal," Tara echoed, then asked. "Uh . . . so Nikki?"

"Yeah?"

"What do we do at slumber parties?"

"Eat, stay up all night, watch mushy movies, paint our nails, talk about people we don't like and hot boys."

Tara grinned. "I can do that."

"This is going to be the best slumber party ever," Nikki said.

The bell rang.

Everyone still in the lunchroom started scrambling, dumping their scraps and trays and heading for the next class.

The rest of the day passed without incident. Prissy was noticeably absent in the halls, and French Langdon seemed to be missing in action, too, but Tara hadn't given them another thought. She was too focused on telling her uncle Pat about the invitation and wondering what was happening with Flynn.

Tara had supper all ready to eat, but Uncle Pat was late. Then he called to tell her there was a big water-main break just off Main Street and they'd roped in some extra help, including him. It left Tara with time on her hands and a guilty conscience she had yet to address.

Twirp him, Tara.

Tara sighed. "Not Twirp—it's Tweet, and it's still not the right contact. I need to text."

Tex? Isn't that a state?

Tara laughed. "You're thinking of Texas, not text, and before you ask another question, I'm going to contact him. Now."

Be gentle. Henry says he's been crying a lot.

Tears welled. "I didn't help make him feel any better."

So now you will.

Tara's shoulders slumped. "I will try."

She picked up her phone, linked to her contact list, and then hesitated a few moments, trying to figure out what to say then realized there was only one thing *to* say to Flynn.

I'm sorry.

She hit Send, then sat motionless, staring at the screen and praying for an answer.

The house grew so quiet she lost touch with the outside world. She could hear a clock ticking. The scent of macaroni and cheese she'd made for supper was in the air, but the thought of food in her stomach made her sick. She closed her eyes, willing her thoughts to Flynn, wishing he was able to hear her as easily as she connected with him. The tears in her eyes were welling faster and faster until they spilled over. Just as she broke out into an all-out sob, her phone signaled a text.

Shakily, she swiped at the tears on her face before she pulled up the text.

Me too.

Tara answered instantly.

Don't be mad. I can't stand it.

She hit Send. The answer came back just as fast.

I scared you. I understand.

Tara started smiling through tears.

I saw you. I saw all of it.

Flynn's answer said it all.

Wow. I get it.

Tara sighed as she typed and hit Send.

Watch your Mom. Watch your back.

There was a pause before he answered.

Really?

Her eyes narrowed. Please, Flynn, get this.

Really.

The answer was swift.

I hear and I heart you.

Tara gasped. Heart? Love? Did he just say he loved her? She typed her answer, but her finger hovered over Send. Was he saying this because everything was so dramatic and tense, or did he really mean it? She took a deep breath, exhaled slowly, then sent the text.

I heart you, too.

It wasn't like they'd actually said the *real* word face to face. Plus, this was a serious time. They needed to have each other's back.

Satisfied that the monkey of guilt was off her back, she left her phone on the end table and went to finish supper. If her uncle Pat didn't come home soon, she was eating without him. Suddenly she was starving.

If she'd happened to glance out the front window instead of going to the kitchen, she might have spotted a tall guy slipping between an empty house and a stand of unkempt shrubs across the street. But she didn't, and had no idea the man stayed in place, even as it began to rain, until Pat pulled into the driveway and went inside the house. By then it was dark as he hunched his shoulders against the cold downpour and disappeared into the night.

It was pouring by the time Pat pulled his car into the drive.

"Hey Tara, I'm home and something sure smells good," he

yelled, as he dashed inside.

"I'm in the kitchen. Wash up. I'm starving."

She could hear her uncle's footsteps as he hurried down the hall to the bathroom. She glanced at the raindrops peppering the kitchen windows and then began making their drinks and setting the table. By the time Pat came into the kitchen, the macaroni and cheese casserole was on the table and Tara was tossing dressing on the salad.

"This looks so good," Pat said. "Anything I can do?"

"Just sit and eat," Tara said. "You look exhausted."

"I'm just glad I don't normally do that kind of work. I think I'm either too old or not in good enough shape. I am certainly glad we finished ahead of this thunderstorm, though."

Then he pretended to flex his muscles, which made Tara laugh. The end of this day was turning out to be way better than the morning had been.

"Hey, Uncle Pat, Nikki is having a slumber party at her house Saturday night. She invited me and two other girlfriends. Her Mom and Dad will be there and it's a no-boys party. Can I go?"

"Sure you can go. I like Nikki."

"Oh thanks, Uncle Pat. I've never been to a slumber party before. I'm so excited."

Pat paused, then leaned back and stared. "Never?"

"No."

"Why not?"

"Because no one ever asked me," she said, and then realized he was looking at her. "What? Is there cheese on my shirt?"

"I can't help but wonder what else you've missed because of our way of life. I can't decide if I feel guilty or sad or a little of both."

Tara frowned. "You don't apologize ever for how we've lived, okay? You are my world, Uncle Pat. You are the only person who's ever had my back."

The salt shaker lifted off the table and then salted Tara's lap.

"Oh! Hey! Okay, Millicent! Okay! I didn't mean to leave you and Henry out, but obviously you're less of a *concrete* reality in my life, okay?"

Just a reminder to you from Henry and me.

"I get it," Tara said, and brushed the salt off her jeans onto the floor. "Now I'm gonna have to sweep the kitchen again," she muttered.

Pat looked a little anxious. He had finally come to accept the two spirits who were part of their lives, but it was still disconcerting to be reminded in a conversational manner.

"At any rate," Tara continued. "I consider myself blessed to have all of you."

Henry popped up behind Uncle Pat and waved at Tara. She grinned.

Pat grinned back until he realized she was looking above his head, not at him. "Is one of them behind me?" he whispered.

Tara laughed out loud. "Whispering doesn't work, Uncle Pat. They're not deaf, and he's right behind you."

"He? Oh, you mean the guy . . . Henry?"

Tara giggled. "Yeah, the guy."

Pat had enough of discussing spirits and shoveled another bite of macaroni and cheese into his mouth and chewed.

"This is really good," he said, and kept on eating, as if ignoring their existence would make them disappear.

Tara hid a smile, and like Pat, finished the meal in relative silence. It wasn't until she got up to carry the dirty dishes to the sink that she realized the wind was getting stronger, peppering the raindrops against the window like bullets. All of a sudden she realized it wasn't raindrops. It was hail.

"Hey, Uncle Pat, turn on the television will you? It's beginning to hail."

Pat frowned as he hurried into the living room, while she began washing dishes.

It's a bad wind.

Tara paused, her hands in the dishwater. Millicent's voice sounded anxious.

"As in a storm?"

Yes.

"Is it a tornado?"

Yes.

Tara's heart skipped. "OMG. Is it going to hit our house?"
Not this one, but many others.

Tara bolted, drying her hands on her pants as she ran. "Uncle Pat! We need to take cover. It's a tornado and it's going to hit Stillwater."

Pat jumped up, wild-eyed and still holding the remote. "But the weatherman hasn't said—"

"Millicent said different. The hall, Uncle Pat. We need to get in the hall. It's the only interior structure without windows."

Tornado sirens began going off all over Stillwater as Pat dropped the remote. In the background, they could hear the television programming being interrupted by a tornado warning. Tara hit the floor and pressed herself up against the wall as close as she could get while her uncle Pat threw himself on top of her. Within seconds the wind had turned into a whine strong enough to rattle the windows in the house.

"I'm scared, Uncle Pat."

Pat wrapped his arms around her. "I'm right here, baby girl. Don't worry. I won't let anything happen to you."

Tara closed her eyes.
You're safe.
What about my friends?

Millicent didn't answer, which made things worse all over again.

The whine escalated. Tara could hear limbs breaking and car alarms going off. She was shaking so hard her teeth were chattering.

All of a sudden the whine turned into a whistling roar and the power went out. There was the sound of breaking glass as her uncle shifted his entire body weight on top of her while the storm ripped through town like a runaway train, pulling roofs off of houses, leveling others in its path, destroying lives and neighborhoods without prejudice.

Tara didn't know she was screaming until Uncle Pat pulled her to her feet and gave her a quick shake.

"Honey, it's passed over us. It didn't hit us. We're okay."

Tara took a deep shuddering breath. "But it did hit. It hit the town. Bad. I don't know why, but I need to call Nikki. Where's a flashlight? I've got to find my phone."

The house was momentarily lit from flashes of lightning as she ran into the kitchen, then into the living room, frantically searching in the dark. Outside, she could hear a different sort of siren as police and rescue workers were dispatched. Finally, she found her phone between cushions on the sofa. Her hands were shaking as she called Nikki's cell. The call rang and rang and just when Tara thought it was going to voicemail she heard Nikki's voice.

"Tara! Are you alright?"

"Yes, are you? Is your family okay?"

Nikki started to cry. "We're all home but Rachelle. She was at her friend's house and no one is answering."

All of a sudden Tara felt like she was choking. "She's choking, Nikki! Wherever she is, she's choking!"

Nikki gasped. "She has asthma! You didn't know that, did you?"

"No, but you need to take her meds and find her. Find her fast."

The line went dead.

Tara dropped the phone in her pocket and looked up as her uncle came through the living room with a flashlight. "Something bad is happening to Nikki's younger sister. I told them she's choking, but I couldn't see where she was."

Pat put his arms around her. "You did your job to warn them. They'll do their job and find her. I'm going outside to look around."

He must not go out.

Tara grabbed his arm. "Wait. Millicent said not to go out."

Pat frowned. "But I—"

Live power line in your yard.

"OMG! Uncle Pat, she says there's a live power line down in our yard."

Pat raced to the doorway and shined his flashlight out into the yard. Even in the rain, he could see the broken wire sparking as the wind blew it about.

"I'll call the city . . . and tell Millicent I said thank you."

"Seriously, Uncle Pat. I keep telling you, they can hear you."

He's welcome.

"She said you're welcome," Tara muttered, then jumped when her phone began to ring. She looked at Caller ID and wanted to cry all over again.

It was Flynn.

"Hello."

"Moon girl! I've never been so glad to hear a voice in my life. Are you all okay? We've been watching the weather from my uncle's house in Ardmore. Did that twister hit town?"

Tara started to cry all over again. "Yes. Our house is still in one piece but there are sirens all over town. Nikki's sister, Rachelle wasn't home and she's in trouble. I just don't know for sure what kind. They're looking for her. There's a hot power line down in our yard so we can't get out, and I don't know how bad the neighborhood was hit."

"Thank God, you and your uncle are all right. Mom says to tell you she said prayers."

Tara swiped at the tears on her face. "Tell your mother they worked."

"Tara . . . hey—"

The call began skipping. "Flynn! I can't hear you. I'm losing—"

And just like that, the call was lost. "Dang it," Tara muttered.

"Who was that?"

"Flynn. He was calling to check on us. He said his mom was saying prayers for us here."

"I gave the city dispatch the skinny on the hot wire. They said the far north side of town was the hardest hit. They'll be out when they can."

She nodded, then wrapped her arms around his waist, buried her face against his chest, and started crying all over again.

"I know, honey, I know. This is a scary situation all around. We have a tree down in the back yard and big limbs down in front, and there's a broken window in the utility room. I think there's a small piece of plywood in the bottom of the utility closet that might be big enough to nail over that window until we can get the glass replaced. Wanna come hold it up while I nail it?"

She nodded.

"That's my girl. Come on, Tara. Whatever's happening, we'll do what we always do. We'll get through it together."

The next hour passed in a blur. They got the plywood nailed over the broken window, then the broken glass swept up and water mopped up from the floor where the rain had blown in. As they moved back through the darkened rooms to the front of the house, an ambulance drove past with the lights on disco and the siren squalling in intermittent rhythm. Police cars were going up and down the streets with searchlights flashing on the houses they passed, looking for people in need of immediate help.

Pat went outside on their porch with his flashlight and shouted down a neighbor who was about to come check on them.

"Stop! Stop! Hot wire down!" he yelled, waving his flashlight toward the sparking line.

The man saw the hot wire just in time and backed off before checking in at another house.

From what Pat could see, the houses on both sides of the street appeared to be standing, but they would need daylight to see the true impact.

Tara came out with his coat and made him put it on, then went back inside out of the cold. She kept waiting to hear from Nikki, yet was afraid of what she'd hear. Millicent and Henry were suspiciously absent, which wasn't all that unusual. When the atmosphere was disturbed, they seemed to have more problems moving back and forth between dimensions.

About two hours later, a utility vehicle pulled up in front of their house. Another hour later, the hot wire was no longer an issue, and the wires had been restrung from the pole to their house. At least they were ready to receive power once the city got it back up again. As soon as their house was secure, Pat left to help with a search and rescue team, leaving Tara on her own.

She was sitting on the sofa and praying for daylight when her cell phone suddenly rang. When she saw Caller ID, she was almost afraid to answer.

"Nikki?"

Nikki's voice was shaking. "You saved my sister's life tonight. I don't know what to say to you, other than I love you so much."

Tears welled all over again. "You found her."

"Yes. The house where she was staying was hit. They were in their cellar, in the back yard. Debris from the house fell on the cellar door and they couldn't get out. She started having an asthma attack and her meds had gone up with the storm. If Daddy hadn't gotten there when he did with her meds and an extra inhaler and helped their neighbors pull the debris off the door, Rachelle wouldn't have made it. There are no words to thank you enough."

"Thank God," Tara whispered.

"Yes, thank God and that wonderful gift He gave you. I gotta go. I just wanted you to know we're okay."

"Yeah, okay," Tara said, then curled up on the sofa, pulled the afghan over her shoulders and cried herself to sleep.

Chapter Four

The rain was over. The sky was already turning a muddy shade of gray in the East as dawn drew near. Tara woke up needing to go to the bathroom and was momentarily disoriented at finding herself on the living room sofa instead of in her bed.

And then she remembered. Stillwater had been hit by a tornado last night. She sat up, rubbing the sleep from her eyes and combing her fingers through her hair. The power was still off, but at least toilets flushed. She ran a brush through her hair, brushed her teeth, then moved toward the kitchen to find something for breakfast.

Uncle Pat still wasn't home, but she didn't think anything of it other than she hoped he was being careful. He was all she had and couldn't think about ever losing him.

The house was cold. She reached for the thermostat to turn it up and then remembered, without power that wouldn't be happening either, so she backtracked to her bedroom, pulled a sweatshirt over her t-shirt, put on some heavier socks and some house shoes before going back to the kitchen.

The stuff in the refrigerator was still safe to eat, but if the power was off much longer, they'd be throwing out food. With that in mind, she chose a leftover piece of pizza, poured a glass of milk and carried them to the living room, eating as she went.

It was almost light enough to see everything now. She walked out onto the front porch to check the neighborhood. There were shingles missing on roofs, small storage buildings that had been in peoples' back yards the night before were scattered about—some in pieces in the streets, while another had been set down without a scratch in a yard four houses down. Trees were down everywhere, but people were already out with chainsaws cutting them away so the residents would have access in and out of their driveways and rescue vehicles could get up and down the streets.

She ate the pizza all the way to the crust and then threw it out into the yard for the birds, downed her milk, and was on her way back inside when she heard the sound of a speeding car. She turned just as an SUV slid sideways then turned up her driveway. As it slid to a stop, her heart skipped a beat. She already knew something was horribly wrong before she recognized the driver as Nate Pierce, the geologist who'd helped her find the body that had been buried in their back yard.

He got out shouting her name. "Tara! Tara!"

He jumped on the porch and grabbed her by the arms and just like that she was sucked into the panic and the fear he was feeling. He was wet and muddy and there was a tear in the knee of his jeans. She could see dried blood on the skin beneath. He was crying, and she knew he didn't even know it.

"Please, my sister's house was hit by the storm last night. We've looked all night and still can't find her daughter, Gracie. She's still a baby, not quite two and—"

She didn't need to hear anymore. "Give me fifteen seconds. I need to change my shoes."

She dashed into the house, kicking off her house shoes as she ran, stomped her feet into a pair of old cowboy boots, put on her all-weather coat and headed for the door. With her phone in her pocket and her house keys in her hand, she locked the door behind her and then they were gone.

They didn't talk again until Nate had backed out of the driveway. He kept trying to control his emotions as he talked, but Tara could tell by the tremble in his voice how distraught he was.

"I know I'm asking a lot but we're at our wit's end and I knew we needed a miracle. That's when I thought of you."

Tara's heart sank. "I can't perform miracles, Nate."

He shook his head. "I know, I know. I said that wrong. We just need to find her no matter . . . no . . ."

Tara touched his arm. "Stop talking. You don't need to explain. I know what this means to you. It's like losing your wife and daughter all over again. I owe you one, but I would still be doing this, okay?"

He stomped the accelerator, driving around storm debris without care for the deep scratches being left on his car, taking alleys instead of streets when the roads were blocked.

"I need to let Uncle Pat know where I'm going," Tara said.

The phone rang twice before he answered. "Tara, are you alright, honey?"

"I'm okay, Uncle Pat. Are you still with search and rescue?"

"Yes. It's pretty gruesome. Is the power still off at home?"

"Yes. Listen, Uncle Pat. Nate Pierce just came and got me. His sister and her family live on the north side of Stillwater. The storm hit their house. Their daughter is missing. They've been looking for her all night. I'll be with Nate if you need me."

"Oh honey, I don't think—"

"I have to, Uncle Pat, and you know it."

She heard him sigh. "Yes, I know. Just be careful."

"I will. You, too."

She dropped her phone back in her pocket.

"Is he upset with you?" Nate asked.

"No," Tara said, and then gave Nate a closer look. His thick black hair was matted to his head from a combination of drying mud and rain. His clothes were torn and there was a huge bruise forming on the side of his face. "You were caught in the storm, too, weren't you?"

He shrugged.

She touched his arm and saw everything. "It's all gone, isn't it?"

He sighed. "It doesn't matter. They are just things. We need to find Gracie. She's just a baby. Even if she's . . . if she's not . . ."

He couldn't finish the sentence and Tara wouldn't do it for him. She wasn't ready to face what was ahead of them. Not yet. She needed to be on-site before she could really connect, and even then it might be too late.

Millicent. Henry. Where are you guys?

There was no answer, which scared Tara even more. She

didn't often walk this path without them, but today it seemed that she would.

Nate drove as fast as he could, but the farther north they drove, the worse the devastation.

"Oh good lord," Tara whispered.

Nate glanced at her just as she turned to look at him. In that moment, Tara's panic shifted and she felt a wave of comfort wash through her. Nate Pierce was a very old soul. She didn't know what that meant to the situation at hand, but it was oddly comforting. She took a deep breath and then exhaled slowly.

We're coming, Gracie. Can you hear my voice? Hold on, baby girl, help is on the way.

When Nate turned into what had once been a housing subdivision, it was obvious it had been in the direct path of the storm. It was less than ten minutes from her house to this side of town, yet it looked like another planet. There were holes in the ground where trees had once stood, an occasional fireplace rising up on a bare foundation like a stake marking the spot where the house used to be. The trees that were still standing were denuded of leaves, their skeletal branches stripped of bark and reaching toward heaven, as if begging for help.

The backend of the occasional vehicle could be seen beneath piles of debris that had been houses, but it was the people who broke her heart. Some were walking up and down the streets calling out names. Others were digging through what was left of their homes.

She saw her first dead man standing beside the upturned roof of a house. She knew he was waiting for someone to find his body before he moved on. She saw the shock on his face when he realized she could see him.

I'll be back, she promised silently, and then looked away as Nate turned a corner and drove down yet another street before coming to an abrupt stop.

"We're here," he said.

Tara got out, her legs shaking, her heart pounding. The

place was still filled with energy from the storm. She could hear screams and feel pain and fear from when it had actually happened.

When Nate grabbed her hand, it grounded the vibes, which helped her focus.

"Careful," he said, guiding her around a sodden mattress lying on the ground.

They stopped in front of a half-dozen people who were sitting on a curb. The three women were crying. When the little boy with them saw Tara, he hid his face in his mother's lap. The two men were in the same shape that Nate was. They all looked like they'd been to hell and got lost on the way back.

"Tara, this is my family. My father and mother, Martin and Naomi Pierce, my sister, Sally Washoe, and this is my sister, Delia Littlehorse, her son, Mico, and her husband John. It's their daughter Gracie who's missing."

Delia stood.

Tara felt the devastation of them all as surely as if she'd lived it. "Tell me what happened," she said.

"She was in my arms . . . and then she wasn't," Delia said, and then collapsed, sobbing.

Tara knelt in front of her. "I need to touch you. It helps me lock into the right vibe."

Delia grabbed Tara's arms. "Find her. Find my baby. Wherever . . . however . . . I beg you."

But Tara didn't hear a word Delia Littlehorse was saying. She was already in Gracie's head, too scared to cry. When Delia turned loose, Tara fell backward onto her backside then scrambled to her feet, staggered a couple of times as she turned in a circle, then felt the pull and started walking.

"Tara, do you—"

She held up a hand for silence and the people behind her went quiet. Her steps were long and strong, while theirs were stumbling and weary as they followed her.

Within moments she was far ahead of them, but she could hear something they could not. She could hear Gracie's voice. She was calling for her mama. What scared her most was that she couldn't tell if Gracie was still in this world, or if she'd already crossed into the next. All she could do was follow the sound.

Mama.

She began to run, past one block where men with chainsaws were clearing paths in the street, then past a second where a church van was distributing bottles of water.

Mama. Mama.

She stopped in the middle of an intersection strewn with debris then turned left, bearing northeast to the swiftly rising sun. She ran past search crews and a passing ambulance, past a crew of firemen trying to put out a fire.

Mama.

The voice was louder now, which meant she was getting closer. Tara ran another block and then into what appeared to be a park, but the swing sets and teeter-totters had been upended and twisted into each other until there was nothing but a lot full of shattered plastic and twisted metal.

Mama. Mama.

She stopped to catch her breath and then closed her eyes. *I hear you, Gracie. Keep talking to me.*

When she started walking again, she went all the way through the park to the other side into what was left of a large stand of shade trees. Just as she entered the woods, the worst happened.

Gracie's voice was suddenly silent.

"No!" Tara screamed, and began running from one pile of debris to another, tearing through limbs, pulling aside pieces of corrugated iron and insulation from houses, but there was no child, alive or dead.

All of a sudden a chill ran through her body. She stopped, took a deep cleansing breath and made herself focus, and just like that the answer came.

Look up.

And she did, straight up into the branches of an old spreading Oak tree recently denuded of leaves, to the fork high above her head and the tattered blanket waving in the wind that had caught among the limbs.

The branches were thick and forked in such a way that from where Tara stood, the blanket almost looked like a hammock.

Suddenly the hair on the back of her neck began to crawl. She could hear whimpering. And when she saw a tiny hand appear over the edge of the blanket, she gasped.

She spun to look behind her. Nate was a good block away, maybe farther, and the family even farther away than that. She didn't dare yell at Nate for fear the sound of her voice would make the baby move and fall. She heard the whimper again and knew there were no seconds to spare.

There was a moment when she wished she was wearing tennis shoes instead of boots, but that was her only hesitation. She shed her raincoat, reached for the lowest limb and pulled herself up. Then little by little she began climbing, using the spreading limbs as her pathway to Gracie.

It felt like forever, but she finally reached the fork in the branches where the blanket was caught. She pulled herself up, then peered over, straight into the face of Gracie Littlehorse.

The toddler was covered in mud. Her rain-soaked clothes were bloodstained and beginning to dry, but when she saw Tara, she lifted her arms as if begging to be picked up.

Tara hesitated for fear she'd make matters worse in case the baby had broken bones, but Gracie was moving her arms, trying to kick the blanket off her legs and she was moving her head from side to side, as if trying to see where she was at. It was all the proof Tara needed that her neck and back were not broken.

Tara lifted her up into her arms. Gracie wrapped her arms around Tara's neck so hard Tara could feel her trembling from shock.

"I've got you, Gracie. Don't be scared. You're okay now," Tara said, patting the toddler's frail, muddy back.

From this high up, Tara had a bird's-eye view of the storm's path. She couldn't believe Gracie had been carried this far by the storm and be alive, and yet here she was.

She looked off in the distance and waved. Nate saw her and waved back, but he was running—his aches forgotten—his exhaustion a thing of the past. She leaned back against the limbs and began patting Gracie's back.

"You must be a very special girl, Gracie Littlehorse. You flew with the storm last night and lit in this tree just like a bird to roost."

Gracie whimpered.

Tara kept patting her back. "I know, honey, I know. Uncle Nate is coming. Your mama is coming and your daddy, too. It's going to be okay, little girl. You'll see."

Minutes later, Gracie Littlehorse's family surrounded the tree, all of them talking and crying at once. It was Nate who silenced them.

"Hush," he said. "The louder you are, the more Gracie will struggle. She's alive by the grace of God. Let's keep her that way."

Gracie still had a death grip on Tara's neck. There was no way she could hold onto the child and climb down at the same time.

"I don't think I can get down with her," Tara said.

Nate looked up. "Don't move. We'll come up to you."

The family was so focused on getting Gracie down they didn't notice the rescue was being filmed by a news crew from an Oklahoma City television station that had come down to cover the damage.

Nate went up the tree first. John Littlehorse started up the tree behind Nate, with Nate's father, Martin, going up behind John. They kept climbing until they were spaced up in the branches like members of a bucket brigade.

When Nate reached Tara he was so elated his heart felt like it was pounding out of his chest. He kept touching Gracie's muddy little body, just to reassure himself this wasn't a dream, then looked at Tara, in awe of what she'd done.

Tara sighed. "I told her she flew with the storm last night and came to roost like a little bird. She won't let go." Tears began to roll down Tara's face. "Oh Nate . . . she's so scared. I can feel her little heart beating all the way to my bones."

He swallowed past the lump in his throat and looked down. John was just a couple of branches below him, and his father,

Martin, was standing on the lowest branch, about six feet above the ground, ready to hand the baby off to Delia, who waited below.

He looked off in the distance. His Mother and his nephew, Mico, were still over two blocks away, but it was time to get this done.

He put his hand on Gracie's back. "Gracie . . . it's Uncle Nate. Wanna go see Mama?"

Gracie was still holding onto Tara, but the familiar voice and the word Mama got her attention. "Mama?"

"Yes, baby girl. Come to me."

In the end, he had to tear her arms from around Tara's neck, and when he did, she began to scream. There was no soothing her—no talking to calm her. She cried all the way down, from Tara to Nate—from Nate to John—from John to Martin—and finally from Martin to Delia. The moment she was on the ground and in Delia's arms, a cheer went up from the news crew.

That's when the family realized the rescue had been filmed. The news crew had already alerted an ambulance that a baby had just been found alive up in a tree and it was enroute to the scene to transport her

Tara was the last to climb down, and when her feet touched ground, she was shaking.

Nate threw his arms around her and hugged her fiercely. His body was trembling as much as his voice. "I will never be able to repay you," he said, as he reluctantly turned her loose.

Tara combed her fingers through her hair, her voice shaking from emotion. "Payback isn't how this works."

"I know, but you know what I mean. Come on. I'll take you home."

"I can't go home."

Nate frowned. "But—"

Tara picked up her raincoat and put it back on, shivering as the coat sheltered her from the chill wind.

"Someone else is lost. I made a promise to help the searchers find him."

Tara started walking and Nate followed.

"I don't understand. When did you—"

"There's a body trapped beneath a roof. The man's spirit is still there, waiting to be found. He won't cross over. He knows I saw him. I told him I'd be back."

Nate was speechless. "I never thought—" Then he began looking around. "Are their others? I mean—"

Once Tara was no longer focusing on Gracie there were voices coming at her from every direction.

"All I can handle is one at a time."

"I won't leave you," Nate said, and then couldn't bring himself to look at her. The devastation in her voice was enough for him to know what this was doing to her, and he was right.

Tara was shutting down her emotions. She already knew it was the only way she'd be able to get through this. Millicent was absent, and Tara hadn't seen Henry at all. The energy of what had happened here still lingered to the point that it was beginning to feel like she was walking in mud. Her legs felt heavier with every step. It was good she wouldn't be doing this alone.

She started walking, following the pull of earth-bound spirits and walked until she saw the roof lying upside down and the spirit beside it.

When he saw her, the relief on his face was evident.

You came back.

Tara nodded. "I told you I would. I'll tell them where you are."

My name is Tom Lewis.

"Tom Lewis. I'll tell them," Tara said.

The light. It's for me, isn't it?

Tara nodded. "You can go now. I won't leave until they find you."

And just like that, the spirit was gone, absorbed within the flash of light that she'd glimpsed.

Tara pulled out her cell phone and turned to Nate.

"Do you know the name of this street?"

He looked around for a street sign, but they were either

bent to the ground or completely missing. Finally, he noticed a daycare sign on the opposite corner.

"No, but we're on the same street and just a little west of where the Little Toddler Day Care used to be."

Tara called the police but kept getting a busy signal. That left her with no other option than to call her uncle again. He answered quickly.

"Hi honey. Did you find the girl?"

"Yes, but now I need your help for something else. Is there a rescue crew anywhere close to the north side of Stillwater where the Little Toddler Day Care used to be?"

"Hang on, honey. I'll find out."

Tara looked back at Nate. "He went to ask."

Nate kept staring at the roof and the debris. "I don't see the body anywhere."

"He's under the roof," Tara said, and pulled her raincoat a little closer up under her chin.

He shuddered and looked away.

"Tara, are you still there?" Pat asked.

"I'm here, Uncle Pat."

"There's a crew heading your way right now. It'll be a few minutes, no longer, okay?"

"Yes, thank you. I have to go."

She dropped the phone back in her pocket and turned her back to the wind. "Help is on the way," she said, then turned and looked across the street.

"What is it?" Nate asked.

"Another voice. Watch for the crew, will you? I'll be right back."

Before he could stop her, Tara was running across the street. Someone was trapped, but she wasn't sure where. Then the moment she touched the debris, in her mind she saw a face—and felt a heartbeat. This one was alive.

"Nate!"

He heard her and came running. "What's wrong?"

"A woman is trapped in here and she's alive. Help me look."

He stopped her. "No, you're gonna get yourself hurt. Look. There comes the search crew. We'll tell them, okay?"

A truck pulled up on the street. The driver, a man named Joe, hit the brakes as the crew in the back jumped out.

Tara ran to meet them and pointed to the upturned roof. "There's a body underneath that roof. The man's name was Tom Lewis. But there's a woman trapped across the street who is still alive. We need to hurry. She's in shock."

"Where is she?" Joe asked, as they moved toward the wreckage.

"I'm not sure. I just know she's here."

Joe stopped. "Look, kid, this is serious business. We don't have time for jokes."

Tara felt sick. "I'm not joking, please. You have to believe me."

Then one of the men from the crew stepped forward. "Hey, I know you. You're Tara Luna, aren't you?"

Tara nodded.

"I helped dig up that body in your back yard. I get where you're coming from, kid. Just point the way. We'll do the rest."

"What are you talking about?" Joe asked.

"Trust me. She's the real deal," the man said. "So we need to start looking. If she says someone is alive in this mess, then it's true."

They began moving through the debris, looking under collapsed walls, behind an overturned vehicle, everywhere there was a place to look, and then all of a sudden someone shouted.

"I've got her! She's in a bathtub underneath this wall and mattress."

Tara backed off. She was done here.

Nate put a hand on her arm. "Can I please take you home now?"

Tara shook her head and walked away, already locked onto a faint cry for help that only she could hear.

Hours had passed since Tara had found Gracie Littlehorse.

The search crew her uncle was with caught up with her before noon and was now following her as she marked locations where bodies would be found and radioing in for help when more than manpower was needed to get to trapped victims. No one questioned the reason they were following the directions of a kid any longer. She'd made a believer out of all of them after the third hit.

They had just pulled a teenager and his little sister from a closet where they'd been trapped when Nate turned to look for Tara and saw her sitting on the curb.

"Tara?"

She didn't answer him, and when he touched her shoulder, she shuddered and moaned.

"That does it," he muttered. "You're going home. I gotta find your uncle."

Tara didn't hear him. She was tired—so tired, and the voices were all too loud for her to block any longer.

A passing police car came to an abrupt stop beside her and Detective Allen jumped out.

"Hey kid, are you alright?" he asked, looking around for her uncle when she didn't answer. When he saw them coming, he waited.

"Is she hurt? Do I need to call an ambulance? What happened here?" he asked.

"She's been helping locate victims for the past seven hours and she's hit a wall. We need to get her out of here now," Nate said.

"I'll take her home," Allen said.

"Can you drop me off at the City Barn on your way?" Pat asked. "That's where my car is parked."

"Hop in," Allen said.

But Tara wasn't hopping. In fact, she was past walking. When Pat started to help her up, her legs went out from under her. It was Nate who carried her to the police car, and it was Nate who quietly watched them drive away.

Chapter Five

Detective Allen pulled up in Tara's drive.

"We're here, kid. Just hang on. Your uncle is right behind us."

Tara blinked. She was home. She stared at Detective Allen without a single memory of how she'd come to be in this car, which was weird. The last thing she remembered was the rescue team finding that teenager and his little sister in a closet, hearing the boy asking if they'd found his mom and dad, and knowing their parents were alive and already in the hospital. She had tried to find the words to say it, but the ability to communicate with the living was momentarily gone.

Allen repeated himself. "Your uncle is on the way."

That's when she realized she needed to get out of the car.

"I have a key," she mumbled, opened the door and was out and stumbling up on the porch before he could help.

"Dang hard-headed kid," Allen muttered. After his last visit here when her ghost had gotten all mad at him and Rutherford, he was afraid to go into the house with her. But his conscience wouldn't let him drive off, so he waited until Pat Carmichael got home before he left.

Inside, Tara was bent on only one thing. She stripped off her filthy clothes and then stood naked in her room, shaking with exhaustion as she dug through her jewelry box for her necklace with the St. Benedict's medal. Her fingers were trembling as she put it on, and then stumbled across the hall into the bathroom. When she realized the power was back on, she was just grateful the water would be warm.

She sat down on the side of the old claw-footed tub and began running a bath then crawled into the depths, clutching the medal. The voices were growing dimmer as she leaned back and closed her eyes.

Suddenly she heard footsteps running down the hall and then Uncle Pat calling her name. "Tara! Tara! Where are you?"

"I'm in the tub, Uncle Pat."

"Are you okay?"

Tara clutched the medal tighter. "I will be."

"I'm going to make us some soup. You need to eat something."

The thought of food made her nauseous, but she knew he was right.

"I'll eat later, okay?"

"Yeah, I guess. But you call me if you need anything. You hear?"

"Yes."

"I'm gonna go make that soup now."

The sound of his footsteps faded as he walked away.

The water was only inches from the rim of the tub when Tara finally turned it off, then she leaned back and closed her eyes, again willing herself to a calm place.

All of a sudden, the box of bubble bath salts elevated then tilted. Tara opened her eyes just as a liberal dose of the little pink beads poured into the water.

We came as quick as we could. I always did love a good bubble bath.

Henry popped up at the foot of the tub, waved and then turned his back and sat down on the toilet facing the wall to give her privacy.

Tara rolled her eyes. One ghost on her toilet and the other adding bubbles to her bath—yes, her life was crazy. No wonder the kids called her *lunatic.*

"What happened to you guys?" Tara asked, and realized her voice was shaking.

We tried to get here, but your storm created a vortex. Henry wound up in Fourteenth Century Persia and caused a ruckus in a harem. I was aiming for here and landed in the Middle Ages. Such a disaster, and I have quite an aversion to that period in time. I was burned at the stake then for being a witch. I am ashamed to admit I still hold a grudge.

Tara watched as the water began to churn. Millicent was

making bubbles in her bath like she used to when Tara was little. She glanced at Henry, who was blowing her kisses over his shoulder. And just like that, her life centered.

"I missed you both. It was awful here."

We know. We saw. You were very brave to help as you did.

"I didn't feel brave. In fact, I don't feel much of anything right now except numb."

That will pass. You'll know when it's all better.

"How will I know?" Tara asked.

Why, you'll cry of course. That's what we women do best.

"Flynn is at his father's funeral. Have you seen Michael O'Mara? On the other side, I mean?"

I don't think he's crossed.

Tara gasped, and sat up in the tub, sloshing some of the water and bubbles into the floor. "Why not?"

Something has been left undone.

"Oh lord. Is there a way I can talk to him? It's about that missing money."

I don't know. It may not be your problem to solve.

"But how can Flynn—"

Like I said, it may not be your problem to solve.

"Even though I'm in the middle of the problem?"

I don't know. I don't like how this feels. You need to keep your distance.

Tara flipped bubbles at the sound of her voice. "Flynn's my boyfriend. I'm not keeping my distance from him."

Your uncle is coming. Later, lizard.

Tara rolled her eyes. "It's not, later lizard. It's later gator."

They're both reptiles. I fail to see the difference.

"You rock, Millicent. And you do, too, Henry."

Henry bounced up against the ceiling and then disappeared in increments, beginning head first. Millicent left, too, but with what sounded like a fart, and not her usual "pop," which meant they were both still suffering after-effects of the atmospheric storm.

Tara woke the next morning to sunshine coming through her bedroom window and no memory of eating her supper or going to bed. She rolled over, glanced at the clock and then gasped. It was after 9:00 a.m. She was so seriously late for school.

Then she noticed her bedroom door was open and that there was a note taped to the door.

No school for the rest of the week. Stay away from the storm site. You did enough yesterday. It's not your job to rescue the world.

She sighed with relief, thankful she wasn't going to be late and facing Mrs. Crabtree again. Twice in one week would be a disaster. And Uncle Pat didn't need to tell her she needed to stay away from the area where all the houses had been hit. Yesterday had been the worst.

She went to the bathroom to wash her face and brush her hair then changed into a warm pair of sweats and some fuzzy socks. She turned up the thermostat as she went to the kitchen and found another note from Uncle Pat.

Had to throw out some of the food. Car keys and money are on the coffee table in the living room. I caught a ride to work so you can use the car to get groceries. Be very careful driving. Still lots of debris around. I was very proud of you yesterday.

Love, Uncle Pat

Tara smiled and then saw a pink puff of smoke.

Henry wants to go to the Sonic Drive-in for a breakfast burrito.

Millicent was already trying to arrange Tara's day.

"Seriously Millicent, I don't even see Henry," Tara muttered. "You just want to go look at that cute guy who works carhop on the morning shift."

Then she turned around and saw Henry sitting on top of the refrigerator.

He waved, and then rubbed his tummy to tell her she needed to eat.

"You seriously want to go to the Sonic, Henry?"

He shook his head and pointed at her.

See, he wants to eat.

"He wants me to eat. He said nothing about himself," Tara said.

I remember food. I am certain I would have liked that breakfast burrito, had I ever had the opportunity to taste one.

"I need to make a grocery list and get my shoes."

We have eternity. Take your time.

"Right," Tara said, and then laughed.

It felt good to laugh. There had been moments yesterday when she wasn't sure that would ever happen again.

A short while later, she was on her way to grocery shop by way of the Sonic. Her phone rang just as she finished giving her order. She answered without looking at Caller ID, thinking it would be Uncle Pat.

"Yes, I'm up and on my way to get groceries."

Nikki giggled. "It's me."

"Oh. Hi. I thought you were Uncle Pat."

"I figured. Hey . . . we saw you on TV this morning."

The hair rose on the back of Tara's neck. "You what?"

"We saw you . . . up in that tree with that baby in your arms. OMG, Tara, that was amazing. You had us all bawling our eyes out here. You are a serious hero."

"That was on TV?"

"Yes, and a half-dozen other shots of you with search crews and everything. Are you okay? You looked exhausted."

Tara's mind was racing. "What did they say about me?"

"That you knew how to find people because you were psychic."

Tara's heart stopped. "You are kidding me. Please tell me they didn't broadcast that."

"What? It's wonderful that you can do that and—"

Tara tuned her out. She was in panic mode, already imagining the far-reaching implications of what this could mean, and none of it was good.

"Uh . . . hey, my order is here. I've got to go. I'll talk to you later, okay?"

"Yeah, sure. Call me when you get time. Come over if you want. We're just hanging out today."

"Yeah, I'll call you later."

She dropped the phone in the seat.

The cute guy with your food is here. His name is Andy. Tell him I said hello.

Tara looked up. The carhop was waiting for her to roll down her window.

"Oh, sorry," she said, and dug out her money. "Keep the change."

The guy grinned. "Thanks."

Henry appeared on the seat beside Tara, watching her open the sack with serious intent.

You didn't give him my message, but it is okay. He's cute, but he doesn't have aspirations of furthering his education. What a shame.

Tara sighed. Crazy. Her entire life was lunatic crazy.

Did you get the hot sauce? Henry likes the hot sauce.

"OMG people! I'm not putting hot sauce on this just so Henry can watch. I'm the one who has to eat this and I don't do hot."

Pity. I once—

"Millicent. No. Please. I'm freaking out here right now. The whole world knows I'm psychic now."

Take a bite. You'll feel much better.

Tara stared at the burrito and then peeled the paper back and took a bite.

"I'm chewing, and so far it hasn't done a thing to reassure me that it is okay about my life going to hell."

Henry filched the packet of hot sauce and promptly squeezed it out on a napkin then leaned over, as if trying to smell it, which was silly because once someone becomes a spirit, there is no longer a need to eat or drink.

See, I told you Henry loves hot sauce.

Tara rolled her eyes and then took another bite. It was weird, but in a way, Millicent had been right. The food made her empty stomach feel better even though she still didn't know how to prepare for what lay ahead.

Don't borrow trouble. It will find you in its own time.

"And that's supposed to make me feel better," Tara muttered.

She finished off her burrito and drink and was gathering up her trash when her phone rang again. This time she checked

Caller ID.

It was Flynn. OMG all over again. What do you say to a guy who texted that he hearts you?

Try hello. I find that works best.

Tara frowned. "Hello."

"Hey you," Flynn said. "Are you okay? I saw that piece on television this morning about you helping finding storm victims. That was beyond sick, Moon Girl. Way to go."

Tara sighed. "Thank you. But now the world knows I'm . . . that I can . . . oh, whatever. You know what I mean."

"That you're psychic? Don't worry about it so much. Most of the people who saw that won't believe it, and the few who do probably won't say anything to you about it for fear you can 'read their minds'. You know how people are. Everyone has something to hide."

Tara grinned. "I didn't think about it that way, but you're right. Thanks. You just made me feel way better than I did five minutes ago."

"Hey, making my girl feel better is part of my job."

Tara's smile widened. "Thank you. You're the best."

"I do what I can. So I just called to check on you. I've gotta go. Dad's funeral is this afternoon. We'll be home sometime tomorrow. Don't get in any trouble while I'm gone."

Tara laughed. "I'll certainly do my best. Drive safe."

"We will. You, too."

Tara was still smiling as she backed out of the parking space and headed for the supermarket. She hoped Flynn was right about people not treating her weird. As she drove, she was so focused on the road in front of her that she didn't notice the guy on the Harley a short distance behind her, and it was just as well. Knowing French Langdon was tailing her every move would have sent her right over the edge.

Tara was in the cereal aisle at Walmart when the first person accosted her.

"Hey. Aren't you the psychic girl who found that baby up a

tree?"

Tara's heart stopped. She turned around to see a short, heavy-set man staring at her and waiting for an answer.

"Uh . . . no, I think you have me mixed up with someone else," she muttered, grabbed her box of cereal and headed for the end of the aisle. To her dismay, the man followed.

"You are her. I am good with faces. Look, I won't tell anybody. Just listen to this deal. Since you're psychic and all, they probably won't let you play the Lottery. But if you pick the winning numbers in the 68 million dollar Hot Lotto jackpot and tell me, I'll buy the ticket and split with you 50/50. What do you say?"

"Leave me alone or I'm going to call the manager," Tara muttered.

"But—"

At that point, a box of Crunchy Pops suddenly flew off a shelf and whacked him on the side of the head.

"Hey!" he yelled, and then to his horror the entire top shelf of cereal boxes came down on top of him.

Make a run for it.

"I can't. I don't have everything on the list yet," Tara muttered.

Then do your thing. I've got your back.

Tara glanced down at the list and headed for the dairy aisle, praying she wasn't bugged here, as well. It would be a lot messier to clean up milk and eggs than it was the upended cereal boxes.

She got the milk and a dozen eggs, and was heading for butter and cheese when a woman pushing a cart turned a corner and came toward her.

"It is you," she said. "I saw you a couple of aisles over and wanted to tell you how great it was that you found that baby up a tree."

"I don't know what you're talking about," Tara said, and began grabbing eggs and looking for a wedge of the jalapeno cheese that Uncle Pat liked.

"It's okay. I understand you wanting to keep a low profile. I just wanted you to know that I think you're a real heroine."

Tara refused to make eye contact, found the cheese, and then glanced down at her list.

Green beans and hamburger meat.

She backtracked to the meat department, sorted through the packages until she found what she was looking for, and then headed for the canned vegetable aisle.

To her horror, the same lady was right behind her.

"Hey, I want to ask you something," the woman said, as Tara dumped a couple of cans of green beans into her cart. "My husband is up for a promotion. Could you tell me if he's going to get it or not?"

"Lady. Leave me alone."

The woman frowned. "Look. You owe it to people to use your—"

The loaf of bread in the lady's cart suddenly elevated. The twist tie fell into the cart below as the entire loaf was dumped onto her head. The scream that came out of her mouth could have peeled paint off the walls.

Tara headed toward the checkout stand without looking back.

"What's going on back there?" the cashier said, as she began to scan Tara's purchases.

"I don't have the faintest idea," Tara said, quickly paid and headed for the parking lot.

It wasn't until she got into the car that she began to breathe easy.

"Well, that was fun," she muttered.

Henry popped up on the hood of her car with a big grin on his face, waved, then morphed into the seat beside her as she backed out of her parking space.

She glared. "I'm happy you were entertained," she said, and drove away.

French Langdon was on the far side of the parking lot waiting for her to emerge. As she headed for Hall of Fame Boulevard, he started the car and began following her at a safe distance when his phone rang.

"What?"

"Update me."

"She's been shopping, but I think she's heading home."

"If you see the need, snatch her. We'll worry about the consequences later."

"I don't think—"

"Look. After that piece came out on the morning news, you know where that's going to lead. She's Flynn O'Mara's girlfriend. If she's the real deal, we're not the only ones who might figure out she could find the money."

"I hear you," French said.

"Keep me posted."

As French disconnected, he realized he'd momentarily lost sight of her car, but he wasn't worried. He knew where she lived.

Tara was home putting up groceries when she heard a knock at the door. Still leery after the chaos at the grocery store, she didn't recognize the big Suburban in the drive, but her concern vanished when she opened the door. It was Nikki Scott and her entire family. When she saw Nikki's mother, she knew where the pretty eyes and dark hair came from, but Nikki definitely had her father's smile.

"I know we should have called," Nikki said.

"I just got home. I've been grocery shopping at Walmart. Come in and have a seat."

Nikki was trying to be cool, but Tara could tell she was a little embarrassed, which set off an alert on Tara's warning system. She kept eyeing Nikki's parents, trying to get a read on what was going on, but she'd didn't get any warnings. At least everyone was happy. It couldn't be bad.

"Tara, this is my dad, Rick, and my mom Ann. Guys, this is Tara Luna."

Tara smiled. "It's really nice to meet the both of you. Nikki is the best."

Rick immediately shook Tara's hand. "It's our pleasure,

believe me. Look, Nikki made sure we understood you like to downplay your . . . your abilities, and we get that. But it's because of you that Rachelle is still alive and we can't downplay that."

Ann started to shake hands, too, and then hugged her instead. "You are amazing and so brave. A simple thank you will never be enough for what you did for our family."

Tara immediately locked into her wave of love and felt bereft when Ann let her go.

That's what a mother's love feels like.

Tara blinked back tears.

Rachelle got up and slid into the seat beside Tara, then gave her a hug.

"Thank you for saving my life," she said, and then started to cry.

Tara hugged her back. "You're welcome, honey. I wish I could take credit for being this amazing person, but the deal is that I came this way so I don't know any other way to be."

Not to be outdone, Morgan got up and then dropped a package wrapped in shiny blue paper into Tara's lap.

"Here, this is from all of us, but I thought of it."

Tara grinned. "A present for me?"

Nikki rolled her eyes. "You may not think it's much of a present when you see what it is."

Tara tore off the paper then took a deep shaky breath as she read the words on the framed and, obviously handmade, certificate.

> ***From this day forth, Tara Luna will be known as an honorary daughter and forever member of the Rick and Ann Scott family.***
>
> **—Rick, Ann, Nikki, Rachelle, Morgan.**

"OMG. You guys. You have no idea what a big deal this is for me," Tara said.

"We know what a big deal it was for us to wake up this morning and know Rachelle was safe in her bed," Rick said.

"Thank you so much," Tara said.

Nikki sighed. "After all this, are you still willing to be my BFF?"

Tara laughed through tears. "Yeah, I'll still claim you, if you can handle my lunatic life."

Rick rolled his eyes. "It can't be much worse than me living with five females."

Tara frowned. "Five?"

Rick grinned. "Yeah, the dog is a girl, too."

Tara laughed out loud, which made all the Scott women groan. "Don't encourage him," Ann said. "He already thinks he's a riot."

Tara laughed again.

"Hey, Tara, do you have any plans for lunch?" Rick asked.

"No."

"Then may we treat you? Not all the restaurants are back open for business, but Hideaway Pizza is. I checked."

Tara grinned. "I love Hideaway Pizza. Just let me get my purse and jacket." Then she remembered her Walmart experience and hesitated. "Uh, you might not want to be seen with me."

"Why?" Ann asked.

Tara sighed. "That thing about me that you saw on TV . . ."

"What about it?" Nikki asked.

"It's causing problems. I couldn't get through Walmart for the nuts wanting me to tell their futures and pick winning Lotto numbers."

"For the love of God," Rick muttered. "Don't worry about all that. If anyone bugs you while you're with us, I'll take care of it."

Morgan high-fived Rachelle. "Cool! Maybe we'll get to see Dad thump someone's head."

"Oh, I didn't say anything about assaulting anyone. I just said I'd take care of it, and I will. I'll sic your Mom on them."

All three Scott girls groaned. "No . . . not the wrath of Mom. Not that."

Ann pretended to be irked, but Tara could tell she thought

it was funny.

"Go get your stuff," Nikki said. "I'm starving and we can talk about my slumber party Saturday night while we eat."

Within minutes Tara was out of the house and into the big Suburban with the rest of the Scotts. Her family consisted of her and Uncle Pat . . . and Millicent and Henry, of course, but they didn't require seating space. Riding with this big noisy family was a joy. She rode all the way to Hideaway with a big smile on her face, listening to Rick and Ann talking to each other in the front seat, while Rachelle and Morgan argued with Nikki in the back. It was sort of like being in the hall at Stillwater High during class break. Everyone was talking at once but hardly anyone was listening.

They got all the way through ordering and eating salads before a diner at a nearby table recognized Tara. She was caught up in the conversation and laughing at the disgust on Rachelle's face as Morgan kept sneaking the croutons out of her salad, when Millicent's voice suddenly appeared in Tara's head.

Incoming. Take cover.

Tara turned, caught movement from the corner of her eye and saw the guy at a nearby table jump up and head their way.

"Oh no," she muttered.

Rick heard her. "What's wrong?"

"Don't say I didn't warn you," Tara said, and then the guy was at their table.

"Hey, aren't you that girl who found the baby up in the tree?"

"No, that wasn't me," she said.

He frowned. "Are you—"

Rick stood up. "Back off my daughter, mister. This has been happening all day and it's getting old. Just because she's the right age and has long dark hair, doesn't mean she's that girl."

The man blinked. "Uh . . . yeah, right. I'm sorry. I didn't mean to intrude and—"

And just like that, Nikki's mom entered the conversation

without an invitation. "If you didn't mean to intrude, then why did you ever leave your table," Ann snapped.

"I'm out of work. I just thought the girl might know of a place that was hiring."

Ann's green eyes snapped. "Are you serious? *The girl*, as you called her, is not the local employment agency and you're interrupting our meal. Are we going to have to call the manager?"

"Uh, no, no, I'm sorry."

His eyes narrowed as he looked at Tara. She could tell he still didn't believe them, but they'd backed him off.

"Sorry kid," he mumbled, and then slunk back to his table.

Tara's cheeks were burning and she was blinking back tears.

"Embarrassing," she mumbled.

Nikki elbowed her. "No biggy," she said, and then giggled. "But that's what Dad meant by saying he'd sic Mom on them. She doesn't mince words."

Tara glanced up. Ann's indignation on Tara's behalf was still evident, but Rick was grinning. He winked at Tara and then pointed at the end of the table. "Someone pass me the red pepper flakes. Here comes our pizza."

It was a simple request, but it shifted the conversation back to food, and just like that, the moment was over. It took Tara a few minutes to let it go, but that first bite of pepperoni pizza was seriously good medicine for what ailed her.

By the time the meal was over, the man had already left the restaurant. If there were any others who'd had a similar notion of approaching her, Rick and Ann's intercession had changed their minds.

Chapter Six

As soon as Tara got home, she turned on the television in the hope of catching that film clip everyone was talking about. She needed to see exactly what they had aired if she was going to be able to defend herself. Full of pizza, she curled up on the sofa with the remote in her hand and promptly fell asleep.

Channing Tatum smiled as he helped Tara climb down from the tree. Tara smiled back.
"I'm hungry, how about you?" he said.
"Starving," Tara said.
"You look delicious. I'm thinking about that curve of your neck where it's the most tender. Umm, I can't wait to take a bite."
"Of me? No. Wait. I thought you meant—Help! Zombie hunk alert!"

Tara woke abruptly with a pillow clutched to her neck and her feet tangled in the afghan.

"OMG, pizza overload. What a nightmare."

She threw the pillow aside, kicked off the afghan and turned off the TV. They might show the clip again during the evening newscast, but she wasn't in the mood to veg in front of the TV all day waiting to see it. The day was getting older and she needed to figure out what she was going to make for supper. A zombie version of Channing Tatum had nothing on Uncle Pat who was always hungry. She was on her way to the kitchen when there was yet another knock at the door.

"Now what?" she muttered, as she peeked out the window. Then a big smile spread across her face and she stifled a squeal as she ran to the door.

"You're back."

Flynn grinned as he stepped over the threshold. "Fair

warning. You're about to get a really big hug."

As he wrapped his arms around her, Tara's heart skipped a beat. This was turning into the seriously best day of her life.

"I'm so glad you're okay," Flynn said, then pulled back just enough to meet Tara's gaze.

Incoming kiss.

Shut up, Millicent. I'm not blind.

"Watching that tornado heading straight for town and not knowing who would survive and who would not was scary. I kept thinking how empty my life would be without you, Moon Girl, and I didn't like how that felt."

And then he kissed her. Not a quick hello/goodbye kiss, but a serious, I-heart-you kiss that made Tara's pulse race. Even after they stopped, Flynn didn't immediately turn her loose.

"Are we good now? I mean, no more hard feelings between us about anything?"

"We're better than good," she said softly.

Flynn grinned. "Yeah, we are, aren't we?"

She blushed, but smiled back, and just like that, her world was on course again.

"So, I heard there's no school the rest of the week."

"Yep. The school wasn't hit, but a lot of students' homes were. Is your place okay?"

"Yeah, except for some downed limbs and missing shingles. Mom called the landlord but he was already on it."

Tara tugged his hand. "Come sit and talk to me."

Flynn followed her to the sofa.

"I'm really, really sad for you about your dad. Are you okay?"

His smile shifted. "I will be. It's a process, you know."

She watched the sadness come and go on his face. "The police still don't know who killed Floy Nettles."

Flynn frowned. "I know. It doesn't really make any sense, you know? Sam and Floy were close. I can't wrap my head around Sam being responsible for killing his brother."

"I don't know who did it, but I do know it wasn't Sam," Tara said. "And you know that means there's someone still out there who wants that money your father hid."

"Yeah, I get that. Mom and I talked. We're paying attention."

"You know what you said about being scared something would happen to me when the tornado was coming? Well that's how I felt when I found out you were missing. That's why I freaked out on you the other day. I don't ever want to feel that again, okay?"

Flynn threaded his fingers through hers. "Deal," he said softly, then gave her hand a quick squeeze. "I promised Mom I wouldn't stay long. We need to get groceries and run a bunch of errands, but I just had to see for myself that you're still in one perfect piece."

Tara stifled a sigh. Flynn sure did know how to make a girl feel special.

"I'm still in one piece," she said.

"And perfect. Don't forget the perfect," Flynn said, and then leaned over and kissed her one more time, but with an emphasis on goodbye. "Gotta run. I'm still off work until next week. Wanna do something tomorrow?"

"Sure, but what? The tornado messed up a lot of the city, and not many businesses have reopened."

"Can we drive through the area where the path of the storm went?"

"We were all over the place yesterday, although now that I think about it, most of the vehicles were rescue-related so I'm not sure. Why?"

"A woman who works the same shift as Mom lost her house. I just wanted to see the neighborhood."

"All we can do is drive that way and see what happens."

He nodded. "How about I pick you up around 11:00 a.m.? As soon as we scope out the storm damage, we can grab some lunch."

"Okay."

Tara walked him to the door, then stood on the threshold waving until he disappeared from view. From the corner of her eye she caught movement across the street, but when she looked, there was no one there. Still, she locked the door behind her as she went back inside. Thanks to that news crew, there was no telling what kind of crazy people were looking for the Stillwater psychic.

French Langdon held his breath, certain that she'd spotted him, but when she went back inside, he relaxed. He was going to have to be more careful. This was no time to blow his cover, and now that the boyfriend was back in town, things were bound to amp up fast. He stayed around until her uncle came home and then left to check in with his boss.

Detectives Rutherford and Allen had just ended another frustrating interrogation with Sam Nettles. The devastation he appeared to be suffering over his brother's murder seemed sincere, and he continued to swear that the only other people who knew about the money had been with him the entire day that Floy had been killed. He told Rutherford and Allen he knew of no one else who might have had a grudge against his brother big enough to want him dead, and that's where the Stillwater P.D. investigation was stalled.

If it had not been for a dead man and Tara Luna's warning, they would have assumed they had all the guilty parties in custody connected with the kidnapping of Flynn O'Mara. But with the psychic teenager's track record for being right, her insistence that Floy Nettle's killer was still on the loose and the O'Mara family was still in danger was something they couldn't ignore. However, until they got a break in the case, there were left scrambling for clues.

Supper was over.

Uncle Pat was taking a shower and Tara was glued to the television waiting for the ten o'clock news to come on. She already knew they were going to air the clip about her helping with the rescue effort again, because they'd gotten a phone call from a television station wanting to do a follow-up piece. Her uncle had quickly refused, but the story was still news. It wasn't as if she wished anything else bad to happen in Stillwater, but she sure hoped something happened soon that would take everyone's mind off of her.

This is exciting, almost like going to the movies. You should make popcorn. We like to hear it pop.

Tara groaned. "It's not exciting that I'm going to be on TV. Not like this. You know what happens when people find out I'm crazy weird."

Henry materialized upside down, which made Tara snicker.

Don't laugh. Henry's sensitive. He's still discombobulated from that storm vortex. We both are.

"OMG . . . Henry's sensitive? What about me? I'm the only one who can see Henry mess up. Everyone in the country has seen my deepest secret revealed."

At that point, Tara heard her uncle coming back down the hall.

"Can it, you two. Uncle Pat is coming back."

He knows about us. What's the big deal?

"Knowing and accepting it are two different things. Please guys, just don't freak him out, okay?"

Ice, Tara.

Tara sighed. "You don't say ice . . . you say, chill. That means calm down."

Whatever. I still say you should make popcorn.

"No, and that's final."

"Who are you talking to?" Uncle Pat said, as he sat down beside her.

"Myself," Tara muttered. "You're just in time. The news is coming on."

He swung his arm over her head and gave her a quick hug. "It'll be okay. You'll see."

Tara's shoulders slumped. "You weren't with me in Walmart, or at the Hideaway when the Scotts took me out to lunch. OMG, Uncle Pat, people were following me in the aisles. They wanted everything from winning Lotto numbers to a place to hook them up with jobs."

He frowned. "You didn't tell me that."

She shrugged. "Well, I am now."

There wasn't much left to say, so they watched, waiting and hoping it wouldn't be aired again, but their hopes were quickly dashed. The news anchors began the broadcast with an update of storm coverage, then updates on the survivors. They led into the film clip of Tara helping the rescue teams with an interview that made Tara cringe. It was an interview with John and Delia Littlehorse in the ER with Gracie.

Tara groaned. Within seconds, their phone began to ring. Pat answered, frowned, and then handed it to Tara.

"It's Nate Pierce . . . for you."

Tara took the phone. "Hello."

"I'm sorry. I didn't know about this interview until a few minutes ago when Delia called to tell me."

Tara sighed. "Yeah, okay."

"It's not though, is it?" Nate asked.

"I haven't seen any of this yet, but I think everyone else in the state did."

"I'm really sorry. Are you being hassled?"

"You could say that."

There was a long moment of silence, and then he added. "I'm so sorry for how it's affecting you now, but I wouldn't change a thing of what you did. You saved my niece's life, and from what I saw of the show that aired this morning, you saved others as well. It's nothing to be ashamed of."

"I'm not ashamed. It's just that, for now, I am officially a freak."

She heard him curse softly, and then heard a big sigh.

"You are not a freak, Tara Luna. You are so special. You have gifts that most of us will never understand, and even fewer will believe. But for our family, you were a blessing. Next time we meet, I hope it's under happier circumstances."

"Yes, me too," Tara said. "Bye."

"Be strong," he said softly, and then the line went dead.

She handed the phone back to her uncle as he pointed at the

screen. Within moments she was reliving the race to find a baby through the lens of a camera she hadn't known was there. She saw herself up in that tree with the baby in her arms—watching Nate and his family climbing toward her, and then relaying the baby down. The story moved from scene to scene, showing a tall, long-legged girl with dark hair blowing in the wind, running up a street and onto a debris-filled yard and the searchers following and rescuing people who had been trapped. They caught the ambulances racing away with living victims as well as transporting others who were not as lucky.

"Oh no," Tara muttered, when the camera suddenly zoomed in on her. Her hair was blowing across her face, there was mud on her forehead and mud and blood on her clothes, and she was crying.

"I don't remember much of any of this," Tara whispered.

"That's just as well," Pat said, and hugged her again, but this time he didn't turn loose. He kept his hand firmly on her shoulder, reminding her that she wasn't bearing any of this alone.

And then they ended the clip with words that sealed her immediate fate.

"There are people alive in Stillwater, Oklahoma tonight because one local teenager, who happens to be psychic, was in the right place at the right time."

"Well, honey . . . I know this is causing you grief, but I want you to know, from my point of view, I am a very proud uncle tonight."

Tara leaned her head against his shoulder and sighed. "Thank you, Uncle Pat."

All of a sudden, Tara sat up straight. "Do you smell that?"

Pat sniffed the air. "I hear something in the kitchen. I hear . . . what the hell? Who's popping corn?"

Tara jumped to her feet. "OMG. Millicent! I told you, no popcorn!"

Pat looked stunned. "Your ghost is popping corn? She can do that?"

Tara rolled her eyes. "I'll be right back."

"Hey, Tara . . ."

"What, Uncle Pat?"

"Well, since it's already popping . . . add some extra butter and bring me a cold can of Pepsi, will you?"

"Sure, no problem," Tara muttered, and headed for the kitchen, following the aroma of freshly popped corn.

She opened the microwave and yanked out the expanded bag and dropped it on the counter.

"Seriously, Millicent? I thought we'd already covered this."

Millicent was suspiciously silent, but Henry was hovering anxiously, which he did when Millicent left him behind to smooth over her messes.

Tara frowned. "Can't you do anything with her?"

Henry shook his head, shrugged his shoulders then blew her a kiss before shooting through the ceiling, still upside down. The last thing Tara saw as he shot out of sight was the grin on his face.

"My life is certifiable."

"Don't forget extra butter!" Pat yelled.

Tara rolled her eyes again. "Seriously certifiable."

The night was dark. The cloudy sky curtained a three-quarter moon to the point that if it hadn't been for the street lights, it would have been hard to cast a shadow. The nightlight in the hall at Tara's house had burned out the right after the storm and they had yet to replace it, leaving the house in total darkness.

Pat was lightly snoring in his bedroom down the hall. The intermittent drip in the old claw-foot bathtub marked off time as steadily as the clock by Tara's bed. The wind was up just enough that the tree limbs on the west side of the house were rubbing against the wall and roof in an annoying, repetitive scratch. Combine all of that with recurring memories of the storm, and it gave Tara the perfect recipe for a night of restless sleep.

She had been tossing and turning from the moment her head hit the pillow, and three hours later, had yet to relax enough to get any actual rest. When a police car went speeding past with sirens screaming, she sat straight up in bed with her heart pounding; her eyes wide with shock.

The fact that Henry was sitting at the foot of her bed was not as freaky as the fact that he was glowing.

"OMG! Henry! What happened to you?" Tara gasped.

Henry shrugged, as Millicent explained.

It's astral dust. I think it gives him a little dash of flash. What do you think?

"Is that on purpose?" Tara asked.

I'm trying to put a good spin on his situation. He got caught up in a comet trail. The least you could do is not stare.

Tara rubbed her eyes sleepily. "Sorry, but it's a little startling to wake up with what amounts to a flashing disco ball at the foot of my bed."

Henry spun off the bed and into the corner, leaving a sparkle trail behind him, then did a little dance step that made her laugh.

"Is he alright?" Tara asked. "I mean . . . is it bad for him to get caught up in a comet trail?"

It's just a matter of realigning energy.

"Why are you two here?" Tara asked. "Is something wrong?"

We don't like the vibe around you. You need to pay attention.

Tara's heart skipped a beat. "Am I in danger?"

We can't tell. Just be careful, okay?

Tara slid back under the covers. "How am I supposed to relax and sleep after a warning like that?"

You're not alone. Just close your eyes.

Tara did as she was told, and moments later felt the mattress give beside her, then a featherweight brush of something across her cheek.

Tara sighed. It wasn't everyone who could claim to have shared a bed with a ghost, and that touch on her cheek was Millicent's version of a goodnight kiss. But it was familiar enough that it lulled her into relaxing, and a short while later, she finally fell asleep.

She woke up hours later to the smell of frying bacon and got up, anxious to get her share before Uncle Pat ate all of it and left her with a bowl of cold cereal, instead.

"Good morning, sunshine," Pat said, as Tara entered the room.

"Hi, Uncle Pat. Did you make enough bacon for me, too?"

"Sure did. Want some eggs to go with it?"

"No, I'll just do toast. Flynn is taking me to lunch today. I want to save room for that."

"So, you and Flynn are becoming quite the thing, aren't you?"

Tara shrugged as she picked up a crunchy strip of bacon and took a bite.

Pat frowned. "You don't want to talk about it?"

Tara looked up. "Hmm? Oh, no, it's not that. I didn't know you were serious."

"Well, I was."

Tara popped a slice of bread into the toaster and pushed it down. "You know I like him, Uncle Pat. I like him a lot, and he likes me. We're cool and we're not doing anything stupid, so save yourself the worry and me the misery of another one of your 'be careful' sex talks, PLEASE. Both of us have plans for college. We're just enjoying life and each other's company, okay?"

Pat grinned. "Okay."

Tara eyed her uncle as he dumped his scrambled eggs onto a plate.

"So, are you and Mona going out again?"

Pat blushed. "I don't know. We talked about it. Why?"

Tara pointed at him with her bacon. "See . . . it feels weird being questioned about your sex life, doesn't it?

Pat rolled his eyes. "I'm an adult. It's different."

Tara snorted lightly, but then her toast popped up, which thankfully changed the subject.

"Do we have any jelly?"

"In the door of the fridge," Pat said.

Tara smeared peanut butter on her toast, added a spoonful

of grape jelly, then took it and the plate of bacon to the table.

They ate in mutual silence until their plates were clean.

"I've got to hurry," Pat said. "Do you mind cleaning up the kitchen?"

"Nope. Don't mind at all," Tara said. "See you this evening, Uncle Pat. Have a nice day."

"See you later, alligator," Pat said.

Tara grinned. Uncle Pat was such an old hippy. "After while, crocodile."

She was still smiling as she cleaned up the kitchen. Since there was still no school, she decided to put in a load of clothes to wash, and so her morning went until it was time to get ready for her date with Flynn.

Flynn was due to arrive almost any minute, and Tara was still waffling about which pair of jeans to wear. She finally opted for the older comfy jeans, as opposed to the newer ones, and dressed quickly. She already had on a long-sleeved red t-shirt, her hair pulled back in a ponytail and her makeup done. All she needed were the shoes and she was good to go.

She was looking for her cell phone when she saw Flynn pull up into the driveway. She poked her head out the door, held up a finger to indicate she needed a minute longer then ran back into the house.

"Oh dang it. Millicent! I can't find my phone."

Between the sofa cushions?

Tara made a quick leap for the sofa, and sure enough, it was there.

"Thanks," she said, dropped the phone in her purse and locked the door behind her as went.

"Hi, pretty girl," Flynn said, as Tara slid into the seat beside him.

She smiled. "Hi, yourself," she said. "So where are we going?"

"Out by the storm site first, then I'm taking you to Texas Roadhouse for lunch."

"I've never been there, but I heard the food is really yummy."

"Yeah, it's the best," Flynn said. "They have an appetizer called Rattlesnake Bites that is so good."

"It's not real rattlesnake is it?" Tara asked.

Flynn laughed as he backed out of the driveway. "No. It's jalapeno peppers and cheese and stuff."

"Oh. That kind of bite," Tara said, and then laughed as they drove away, unaware that the guy on the Harley a block and a half behind was trailing them.

"Show me the tree where you found the baby," Flynn said, as they drove slowly through the ravaged neighborhood.

"It is east of what used to be a neighborhood park."

"Oh, I know that park, or at least I used to. Dang . . . this place looks like a war zone," Flynn said. "How awful is this?"

"Pretty awful," Tara said, shivering slightly. The vibe of the place was still strong enough to make her sick. She pointed. "If you turn here, I think it takes you down by the park."

"Yeah, I think you're right," Flynn said, and a few moments later, Tara pointed. "That's the tree . . . the really tall one with the huge limbs."

"I can't believe a baby actually lived through that."

"Stranger things have happened," Tara said softly.

Flynn reached for her hand and held it. They drove out of the area without talking. It wasn't until they turned onto Lakeview Road and headed east that the mood shifted.

"Are we going to eat now?" Tara asked.

"Yeah. Are you getting hungry?"

She nodded. "I'm not real big on hot stuff, but if you order those rattlesnake thingies, I want to try one."

Flynn laughed. "I'll order those rattlesnake thingies every time just to hear you say thingies."

"Are you making fun of me?"

"Yeah."

Tara laughed. Right now, life felt just about perfect.

When Flynn braked at a Stop sign, a large truck loaded with storm debris pulled out in front of them and proceeded East on the four-lane that was Lakeview Road. A guy in a sports car flew past and began tailgating, trying to pass as Flynn and Tara followed behind.

"That jerk is going to cause a wreck," Flynn muttered.

Tara's heart skipped. Was this the vibe that Millicent had warned her about last night? She tugged on her seat belt just to make sure it was fastened, and gripped the edge of the seat with both hands.

As they drove onto the bridge spanning the south end of Boomer Lake, the driver in the sports car sped up and began to pass the truck in front.

"Holy cow!" Flynn said. "Would you look at—"

All of a sudden, the sports car whipped back into the eastbound lane to keep from being hit head-on by oncoming traffic, and in the process, clipped the back end of the truck. It jarred the truck enough that a large piece of the debris suddenly flipped out of the bed and onto the sports car which was already spinning out of control.

"Look out!" Tara screamed, as the sports car spun toward them.

With traffic on their left and the low bridge railing on their right, they had nowhere to go. The car hit them twice—first on the driver's side fender, then as Flynn's car started to spin, again on the back bumper.

"Hold on!" Flynn yelled, as their car flipped once, then went airborne, over the guard rail, and into Boomer Lake.

Tara came to as the car was sinking nose first into the water and quickly unbuckled her seat belt. If they were going to survive, they would have to get themselves out.

"Flynn! Unbuckle your seatbelt. I'm going to roll down the windows so we can swim out."

Then she saw Flynn, unconscious and slumped over the steering wheel.

"No, oh my God, no!" she screamed.

Frantically, she unbuckled his belt and tried to pull him

toward her, but the steering wheel was too tight against his chest.

"Oh God . . . help me, please," Tara said, as she got down on her knees and tried to reach over Flynn's legs to reach the lever that moved the seat back.

Water was coming up into the car now and it was cold—so cold. The adrenaline in her body made her hands shake as she finally pulled him free, and when she did, he moaned and began coming to.

"Flynn! You have to help me. We have to get out now. Are you ready? I'm going to roll down the windows before it's too late."

"I can't breathe," he groaned. "Help me, Tara, help me."

Tara was crying and praying now as she rolled down the windows. The water came rushing in so fast that she couldn't get Flynn out and she couldn't leave him behind and let him drown. Unless a miracle occurred, they were both going to die. The water was making a strange sucking sound as it gobbled up the car, swallowing it and its contents whole.

Tara began screaming at Flynn, begging him to move as the water rushed up to their chests—then their necks. She was holding Flynn's face out of the water, pushing him as far up as she could until their heads were touching the roof of the car. She couldn't believe this was happening. It was just like her dream. They were going to die. Where was her backup when she needed them?

"Millicent! Henry! Uncle Pat! Someone! Anyone! Help! Help!"

Seconds later, the water was over their heads.

French Langdon was on his Harley and less than a block behind them when he saw the sports car spin out of control. When it hit the car Flynn and Tara were in, he knew what was going to happen. He grabbed his phone and dialed 911 as he watched the wreck unfold.

"911. What is your emergency?" the dispatcher said.

"There is a three-vehicle accident on Lakeview Road on the

bridge over Boomer Lake. Road is blocked. One car with two occupants just went in the lake."

He tossed his phone into the pack on his bike and then revved the engine so fast it ate up the distance between them in seconds. He brought the bike to a sliding stop at the edge of the guard rail on the bridge. He pulled off his boots and jacket, grabbed a tire iron from the backpack on his bike and went off the bridge into the water, even as bystanders were stopping and rushing toward the rapidly sinking car.

He swam to where he'd seen the car sink and then dived down. Within seconds he felt the back bumper of the car and grabbed hold, pulling his way down the side of the car as it continued to sink. When he realized a window was already down, he dropped the tire iron and reached in, felt a shoulder, then hair—grabbed a handful and pulled.

It was Tara.

She came out limp and lifeless, but he wouldn't let himself think she might be dead. He just pushed her up, swimming as fast as he could swim. Within seconds of reaching the surface someone grabbed her out of his grasp. He took a deep breath and went back for the boy.

The car was sinking fast and French was afraid he wouldn't be able to find it again in the murky depths. When he finally felt the fender, he pulled himself down to the open window again and leaned in. As he did, he felt the driver's body float toward him. He grabbed hold of the body, bracing himself against the side of the car and pulled hard. The body came out of the window, floating lifelessly in French's arms. He couldn't see anything, but he knew which way was up, and kicked hard, swimming toward the surface and taking Flynn with him. When they came up out of the water, French gasped greedily, drawing in deep, life-saving breaths of air. But Flynn O'Mara was not moving or breathing.

"I've got him," someone shouted, and took Flynn out of his arms.

French swam toward shore, and then crawled out on his hands and knees before collapsing onto the grassy verge. He could hear the loud, piercing squall of the ambulance pulling up at the end of the bridge, and he'd never been so grateful for the sound in his life.

He rolled over onto his knees then rocked back on his heels to assess the situation. Someone was already giving the girl CPR. As he watched, she choked, coughed, then coughed again and began spitting up water. At least one of them was alive.

He looked toward the boy. Another bystander had begun chest compressions but the arriving EMTS pushed the man aside and began working on Flynn.

French was angry that a speeding driver had caused this, and sad that the kid might not pull through. What a waste—what a colossal waste of a good life. The father had just died, and now it looked the son might join him.

Suddenly, one of the EMTs yelled. "Stop compressions. Check out the bulging neck vein. The kid's got a collapsed lung."

French caught a glimpse of a large needle in the EMT's hand. As he raised his arm and plunged it into Flynn's chest, French looked away, then moved to his bike and grabbed his phone.

"It's me. The O'Mara kid and his girlfriend just went into Boomer Lake. No. It was an accident. I saw it happen and pulled both of them out. Yeah, she's gonna make it. I'm not so sure about the boy. I know. I'm about to make myself scarce."

He put on his boots and coat, then started the Harley and quickly disappeared.

Chapter Seven

Pat Carmichael was working his way down Western Avenue on the last leg of his meter reading route when a sudden burst of wind sent leaves and dust whirling around him. He squinted, ducked his head against the wind and moved a little faster, expecting to walk out of it, but the whirlwind followed him.

"What the heck?"

He stopped, and when he did, the wind stopped blowing.

Frowning, he took another step, and the meter reader he was carrying flew up and hit him in the chin, then dropped to the ground as the whirlwind again enveloped him.

He was on the verge of freaking out, when it hit him. What if this was one of Tara's ghosts? What if something was wrong with her and they were trying to tell him to check in?

He picked up the meter reader then looked behind him, making sure no one was around to witness the fact that he was about talk to himself.

"Look guys . . . I'm gonna take another step. If this *is* you and something is wrong with Tara, make it blow."

He stepped, and immediately the wind and dust were in his eyes and up his nose. His pulse shot up a notch.

"I'm going to take that as a yes. If I'm right, stop the whirlwind crap."

The wind instantly ceased.

Fear shot through him so fast he couldn't think. His hands were shaking as he dialed Tara's number, and when she didn't answer, panic enveloped him. At that point, he called Mona. She answered on the second ring.

"Hello."

"Uh, hi, Mona, it's me, Pat. Just thought I'd check in. How's Flynn?"

"He's doing okay. He just went over to pick Tara up a short while ago. I think he's taking her out for lunch."

"Oh. Well, that's good. She'd been pretty down since the tornado ordeal. Look, I'm on the job, so I won't talk longer. I'll check in with you later, okay?"

"Okay. My sister is here today and we're having lunch. Thanks for calling."

"Sure thing. Later."

He hung up. She didn't know any more than he did, and with no other way to confirm his worst fears, he dialed the police.

"Stillwater Police Department, how may I direct your call?"

"Uh . . . this is Pat Carmichael. I know this may seem a little weird, but I have reason to believe my niece, Tara Luna, might be in trouble. Can you tell me if there have been any accidents involving a teenage girl and boy, or if there have been any calls in to the police, either from her or about her? She would have probably been with a boy named Flynn O'Mara."

"One moment please," the woman said.

Pat was already walking back toward the city truck. The wind was blowing again, but it was at his back, as if trying to hurry him along. He got the message and started to run. A few seconds later, the woman was back on the phone.

"Hello? Sir? Are you still there?"

Pat knew he was out of shape when he realized he could not run and talk at the same time. He stopped again, gasping for breath.

"Yes, I'm here."

"Your niece was in an accident. She's on her way to Stillwater Memorial."

Pat froze. "Oh God, oh God, please tell me that she's still alive."

"I'm sorry, sir. I have no information on her condition, only that she was involved in an accident."

"Was there a young man with her?"

"Yes. They are both enroute to the hospital."

He dropped the phone in his pocket and began to run. The

truck was at the end of the next block, but it might as well have been in the next state. It only took a couple more minutes to get to it, but to Pat, it was an eternity. He kept thinking this was how he'd lost his sister and her husband, and why he'd ended up raising Tara as his own. He wouldn't let himself believe that God was going to do this to him again.

When he got to the truck, his heartbeat was roaring in his ears. He made a call to Mona. When she answered, he didn't waste words.

"Mona, it's me, Pat."

"Hi. What—"

"Just listen. Flynn and Tara were in an accident. They're on their way to the hospital and I'm headed that on my way now."

He heard her gasp, and then the disbelief in her voice

"No! Oh dear God, do you know what happened? Are they seriously injured?"

"I don't know anything more than what I told you. I'm assuming Flynn was driving your car."

"We're on our way. I'll see you there."

He hung up and took off toward the hospital, taking alleys and back roads to keep from getting caught at stop lights. By the time he got to the hospital he was crying, and that's how he entered ER, with tears on his face and Tara's name on his lips.

"My niece was in an accident. Her name is Tara Luna. Where is she?"

The clerk glanced up then checked a chart. "The doctor is attending to her now. Just have a seat and they'll be out when—"

"I need to talk to the doctor now! She has medical allergies they need to know about. Please! Where is she?"

The clerk stood. "Follow me," she said, and led him to a curtained area down the hall.

Pat was in a panic as they hurried past one curtained area after another. Some beds were empty, others were not. He saw Mona and another woman standing just outside a curtained cubicle, caught a glimpse of her panicked expression and his heart skipped a beat. A step later, he saw Flynn lying unconscious and motionless on a bed with half the clothing cut away from his body and a flurry of doctors and nurses working on him. Seeing Flynn like that was like a fist to the gut, imagining Tara in the same condition.

The receptionist suddenly stopped and pointed into Bay 7. When he saw Tara awake and talking, he choked back a sob of relief.

"Tara. Baby girl. Thank God."

Tara was still confused and in pain. All she could remember was Flynn saying he couldn't breathe and then the water coming over their heads. She had regained consciousness in the ambulance with no memory of getting out of the car.

"Where's Flynn? Somebody has to help Flynn," she moaned, and kept pushing at the doctor's hands.

He flipped a light in her eye, watching to see if the pupil contracted normally.

"What's your name, honey?"

"Tara . . . my name is Tara. You have to help Flynn."

He flipped the light in her other eye, talking calmly as he quickly assessed her injuries. "You're in a hospital. Do you remember what happened?"

"We were in the water. How did we get out of the water? Where's Flynn? You have to help Flynn." Then she heard someone else call her name and recognized the voice. "Uncle Pat?"

"I'm here, baby," Pat said. "I'm here." He moved to the foot of the bed so she could see him. Afraid the doctor would run him out, he quickly started to explain. "I'm her family. You need to know she's allergic to codeine. Did she tell you?"

The doctor's eyes widened. "No. Somebody note that on her chart, stat!"

Tara started to cry. "The car hit us, Uncle Pat. It hit us twice. We went into the lake. Flynn couldn't breathe. I held his head above water, but he still couldn't breathe. It's his chest. Something is wrong with his chest."

The doctor glanced at one of the nurses. "They probably

already know that, but make sure," he said.

The nurse hurried away to deliver the message while the doctor continued to assess Tara's condition and treat her injuries. She had contusions on her head and cheek and some shallow cuts on her hands and legs.

"Does she have any broken bones?" Pat asked.

"I don't think so, but we've already taken x-rays and are awaiting results. She was unconscious when they pulled her out of the water, but responded to CPR."

Pat kept patting Tara's foot, unable to believe how close he'd come to losing her.

"I'll be admitting her to the hospital for observation, if no problems pop up, we'll let her go home in a day or two."

Pat kept nodding, trying to absorb everything the doctor was telling him. All he wanted to do was wrap his arms around her, but she was only focused on Flynn.

"Uncle Pat . . . did you see Flynn? Is he alright?"

"I saw him in another cubicle. They're taking care of him, honey."

"Is he okay?"

"I don't know, Tara. His mother and aunt are with him."

"I can't believe this is happening," she said, and started to cry.

The doctor finished his examination and patted her shoulder. "You're a very fortunate young lady. They're going to take you upstairs to your room. Your uncle can go with you, okay?"

Tara wiped her tears as she nodded. "Can I please see Flynn?"

The doctor shook his head. "No, sorry, honey. Not just yet."

I'll do it for you. Don't worry.
Millicent! Where were you?
We brought your uncle.
Really?
Just ask him. He'll explain. You rest. I'll be back.

Tara exhaled slowly, closing her eyes as the tears ran

unheeded down her face.

"I'm here, baby girl."

Pat squeezed her arm and then stepped out into the hall as they transferred Tara from the ER bed to another one and began rolling her toward the elevator to take her up to the room.

Mona and her sister were gone, and the bed where Flynn had been was empty. After what Tara had said about him not being able to breathe, Pat guessed they must have taken him to surgery.

Tara didn't know Flynn had been that close by. She couldn't believe this was happening. How could something that had been so perfect turn wrong so fast? She moaned. Her head and face hurt, her chest hurt, she was sick to her stomach, and the knot in her belly was pure fear—fear that Flynn wasn't going to make it.

"Are you okay, Miss Luna?" the orderly said.

"No," she whispered. "I'm afraid nothing will ever be okay again," and clutched her uncle's hand even tighter.

The bed stopped moving as the orderly paused to press the button for the elevator. She could hear the car rumbling as it traveled down the shaft toward them. Then the door opened and a tall man wearing a long-sleeved white cotton shirt and blue jeans got off. He was standing against the wall as they wheeled Tara's bed into the car, and for a fraction of a second, his gaze locked onto Tara's with such intensity that she lost her breath.

Ghost!

She'd never seen him before, but she knew who it was, and she knew where he was going.

Millicent! He's here! Flynn's father—he's going to Flynn. Does that mean Flynn is dying? Did Michael come for him? Help me! Help me! I can't bear this alone.

I see him. I will observe.

Tara's heart was pounding so fast she felt faint. Just when she thought things couldn't get any worse. OMG.

Two hours had passed since Tara's admission to the hospital, and the longer time passed, the heavier her chest felt. A nurse explained that it was sore muscles from the CPR, and that if she didn't develop a fever or pneumonia from the water that had been in her lungs, she was going to come off as a very fortunate young girl. Exhausted in both body and spirit, she continued to doze off, and every time she woke up, she asked about Flynn's condition. When she woke up again, Pat was sitting in a chair by her bed. "Uncle Pat?"

He sat up straighter. "I'm right here. How do you feel?"

"Weird. Sore. Is there any news about Flynn?"

He shook his head.

"Please, will you go see if you can find anything out? Find the surgery waiting room and see if Mona is there . . . do something. I can't stand this not knowing anymore."

"You can't tell anything with your powers?" Pat asked.

"No, and that's what bothers me. I sent Millicent to find out hours ago and she never came back. She said she helped get you here. What did she mean?"

"Let's just say they got my attention, and once I figured out it was them, I knew something must have happened to you. I tried to call you but you didn't answer. I called Mona, but all she knew was that Flynn had gone to pick you up. After that, I called the police department. They're the ones who told me there was an accident and that you and Flynn were being transported to the hospital."

"I'm glad they did. I was never so happy to see anyone in my life, but I need to know about Flynn. Please go see if you can find anything out."

He frowned. "I don't like to leave you."

"Look at me. I'm fine. Please, it's driving me crazy."

"Okay, but I won't be gone long."

Tara watched him leave, and then pulled the covers up under her chin and tried not to cry. Her head already hurt. Crying would just make it worse.

She leaned over to get a tissue, and when she turned back, Michael O'Mara's ghost was standing by her bed.

She flinched and then frowned, uncertain how this was going to go. She couldn't tell if he was sad or mad, but either way, she wasn't taking the blame for his troubles. She wanted to know about his son.

"Is Flynn okay?"

In surgery.

"Still? Is it bad? Is he going to be okay?"

You see me.

"Obviously."

Will you help Flynn?

"Yes."

Tried to talk to him. He couldn't hear me.

"So talk to me. I see and hear you. Tell me where you hid that stupid money before someone else winds up dead. They kidnapped him you know. They could have killed him."

Don't know you. Don't trust you.

Tara rolled her eyes. "Then what do you want from me?"

He didn't answer, but she could see his frustration. And even worse, he was fading. As she watched, he completely disappeared.

"Millicent! Where are you?"

I'm here, darling. We're both here.

Henry popped up at the foot of Tara's bed. He looked upset.

"What's up with Flynn? His father was just here, but I don't know what he wanted."

He's alive. A rib punctured one of his lungs. They will fix him.

"OMG! He's going to be all right? He's going to live?"

He's alive. I don't know about all right.

"What do you mean?" Tara cried.

He's going to be asleep for a time. How he wakes up, is how he will be.

Tara moaned. "You mean he's going to be in a coma? That they won't know if he has brain damage until he comes out?"

Yes. That is what I am shown.

Tara rolled over onto her side and began to sob. "Why is this happening? We weren't driving too fast. We were being so careful. This isn't fair. This just isn't fair."

Life isn't fair. No one ever said it would be. It is just life.

A nurse entered the room and moved to Tara's bedside.

"My name is Bobbi. I'll be your nurse for the evening. Is there anything I can get you?"

"No," Tara said, and resisted the urge to pull the sheet over her head.

The nurse slipped a blood pressure cuff around her arm. "I am going to take your blood pressure and temp. It won't take long."

Tara closed her eyes. She didn't care what they did to her.

Pat returned as the nurse was taking Tara's blood pressure. He waited until she was gone, then sat down on the side of her bed and reached for Tara's hand.

"So, Flynn is out of surgery and in ICU. I spoke briefly to Mona. She's hysterical, but at least he came through surgery okay. He had some broken ribs, they think from hitting the steering wheel, and one of them punctured his lung, which was why he couldn't breathe like you said. But everything has been reset or repaired. Now he just has to wake up and get well."

Tara needed Uncle Pat's strength to get this said and gripped his hand a little tighter. "He's not going to wake up yet. He's in a coma, and there is no way to know whether he has brain damage or not until he regains consciousness."

Pat was shocked. The news made him sick.

Tara shuddered, too broken to talk anymore. "I love you. I just want to sleep now, okay?"

He kissed her forehead and then patted her shoulder. "I'm so sorry, baby. So sorry. I'll be right here when you wake up."

Her chin quivered. "Don't tell Mona. She'll find out soon enough. "

Pat's eyes were full of tears. He didn't trust himself to speak, so he pulled up a chair by her bed and sat down.

He'd already called his boss. They were bringing his car from work and trading it for the city truck he'd been driving. Someone else would have to finish his meter reading route today. He wasn't budging until his girl went home.

What none of them knew was that, once again, the media had gotten wind of the accident and that it involved the psychic girl who'd helped save lives after the tornado. Before long, flowers began arriving in Tara's room from people they didn't know, praising her efforts on behalf of the city and offering prayers for her and Flynn's recovery. It made her cry all over again. All of this was happening and Flynn didn't know—might never know. It made her heartsick to think that her sweet, funny Flynn might never wake up.

When the nurses began bringing supper trays, Tara couldn't eat. Every time someone tried to cheer her up, she broke into tears all over again. There was no way for her to be happy when Flynn's life was on hold.

At Tara's bidding, Pat had gone back to ICU again, leaving Tara momentarily alone, but not for long. There was a brief knock on her door and then Nikki peeked in.

"Is it okay to come in?"

"Yes," Tara said, and then burst into tears.

Nikki crawled up in bed with Tara, wrapped her arms around her, and cried, too.

"Flynn is in trouble, isn't he?" she asked.

Tara nodded.

"Talk to me," Nikki said.

"He broke ribs in the accident and one punctured a lung. He's out of surgery in ICU, but he's in a coma. There's no way to know if there are going to be other . . . uh, issues . . . until he wakes up."

"I'm so sorry," Nikki said. "I know a little bit about how you're feeling. I went through the same thing when Corey had that seizure and died, remember? The fact that he was revived and is alive today is because of you. We'll never forget it."

Tara's eyes welled. "I hope Flynn wakes up as healthy as Corey did."

"We're just going to assume he will, okay?"

"I wish I could be sure," Tara said.

Nikki eyed the food on Tara's tray. "You should eat some of that."

"I can't. It just sticks in my throat."

"You can eat the pudding and drink the iced tea," Nikki urged, and handed her the pudding and a spoon. "I have stuff to tell you."

Tara sighed, poked the spoon into the pudding and then licked it off as Nikki began filling her in.

"The guy who caused the wreck is in jail. Daddy said to tell your uncle and Mona to get a lawyer and make sure his insurance company knows they're gonna have to pay up."

Tara nodded. "I'll tell him," she said, and poked the spoon back in the pudding.

"They're saying that some dude on a Harley saved your lives. He was the one who went in the water and pulled you both out of the sinking car, but they don't know who he was, because as soon as the ambulances arrived, he rode off."

Tara frowned. "Really?"

"Yeah, really. Do you remember seeing a guy on a Harley before the wreck?"

Tara shook her head.

"At any rate, it's lucky for you guys he was there. School is going to be closed until next Monday and the slumber party is on hold."

Tara felt sad, thinking how she had been looking forward to it, and now it was such a minor event compared to everything else that had happened.

"I'm sorry," she said.

Nikki frowned. "Please. You have nothing to apologize for, and none of us feel like partying right now. Between the tornado and what happened to you guys, we're all pretty down."

Tara set the pudding back on the tray and picked up her tea. Condensation dripped onto her gown as she lifted it to her mouth, but she didn't care, and the cold icy drink felt good going down her throat.

At that point, an aide came into the room with another vase of flowers.

"My goodness, young lady, you're about to run out of room to put flowers. Aren't these pretty?" she said, and then set them down and left.

"Want to see who sent them?" Nikki asked.

"Yes, please," Tara said.

Nikki pulled it out of the envelope and handed it over.

It was from the Littlehorse family.

We are praying for you and your friend. Stay strong. Delia, John, Mico, and Gracie Littlehorse.

She set the card aside. The tornado and its aftermath seemed like a lifetime ago.

Nikki put the card back in the envelope then hugged her. "I'm going home. We all wanted you to know that we love you, and if you need anything . . . anything at all, you just have to do is ask."

"I'm glad you came," Tara said.

"So am I," Nikki said, and blew her a kiss as she left.

Tara looked at the food tray. The scent of the food mixed with the scents from the flowers was almost sickening. She buzzed the nurse and asked her to remove her tray, then rolled over and curled up into a fetal position and closed her eyes. Maybe when she woke up, this would all be nothing but a bad nightmare.

Then she felt a touch on her shoulder.

We're here. You can sleep. You're not alone.

"I love you guys," Tara whispered.

We love you, too.

Tara was awake again, staring at the program on television without actual listening. Visiting hours had just begun because she could hear voices out in the hall; whispering, laughing, crying. Even though it was good that doctors were here to make you better, hospitals sucked eggs.

Her uncle Pat had gone down to the cafeteria to get something to eat, leaving her in a room full of flowers and a rerun of The Big Bang Theory. She didn't feel like laughing and changed channels repeatedly until giving up and turning down the volume.

Every time she closed her eyes, she kept reliving that moment when the water had gone over their heads. It was the most heart-stopping fear she'd ever known. She knew now how they'd gotten out of the car, but it was shocking to know that for a time, she'd been dead, and that if it hadn't been for some people performing CPR, Uncle Pat would be planning her funeral.

It wasn't your time.

Tara heard Millicent's voice, but she didn't answer. Until she got some good news, she didn't want to hear another platitude.

Henry popped up below the wall-mounted television and blew her a kiss, but even that didn't help. All she wanted to do was cry.

Then there was a knock at her door. She tensed as the door swung inward. When she saw who it was, she relaxed.

"May I come in?" Nate asked.

Tara nodded.

Nate walked to her bedside, then stopped and laid a hand on her forehead. "I'm very glad you're okay."

New tears welled. "Thank you."

"I brought you something," he said, and handed her a gift.

Tara's hands were shaking as she undid the wrapping. When she saw what it was, her eyes widened.

"It's called a dream-catcher," Nate said, as he held it up. "It's supposed to hang over your bed, the webbing within the circle catches all the bad dreams, letting only the good ones come through the small hole in the middle."

"It's beautiful," Tara said, fingering the dangling feathers and the tiny colorful beads fastened in the webbing.

"The items on a dream-catcher are meant to be special only to the person to whom the totem is given. This small rock is called a moon rock, and this is not a butterfly, it is a Luna moth. Both the rock and the moth are for your name. The bear claw represents strength. You are a strong woman, Tara Luna. These will be good medicine for you."

Tara looked at Nate. His voice was shaking and there were tears in his eyes. The gift was special, but it was his empathy that meant the most.

"I've been afraid to close my eyes," Tara said. "Maybe this

will make the difference."

Nate glanced at the wall above her bed. There were several plug-ins and plugs where machines could be attached. He hung the dream-catcher over a plastic clip and then stepped back.

Tara turned so she could see. From where she was lying she could see the tips of the feathers still fluttering from the movement. Just knowing it was there made her feel safe—like she'd be protected from the bad dreams she knew would be coming.

"Thank you, Nate. Considering how I first bugged you for help, you continue to be a good friend."

He shrugged slightly, as if embarrassed he would say too much. "Good friends are hard to come by. Just so you know, our church is praying for your friend's recovery."

"Thank you. When I get to talk to him, I will tell him."

"I'm going to leave now. If you need anything, all you have to do is ask."

Tara pointed to the dream-catcher. "Thank you for this."

Nate started to touch her again, and then stopped and waved a hand instead. "Rest well, little warrior."

Tara's heart skipped a beat. Warrior? She liked how that word made her feel.

A couple of moments later the door swung open again. Tara thought Nate must have forgotten something until she saw a woman standing in the doorway. She was a heavy-set, middle-aged woman with hair as red as a Santa Claus suit. The way she was staring made Tara feel like a bug under a microscope.

"Are you Tara Luna?"

"Who are you?" Tara asked.

"Are you really psychic?"

Tara frowned. "Please, go away."

"All I need is—"

The woman stopped, glanced over her shoulder, gave Tara a frantic look and then took off, letting the door swing shut.

"That was weird," Tara said, but then what wasn't crazy these days?

104

As soon as the door closed behind her, she looked up at the dream-catcher, rolled over and closed her eyes, and finally fell asleep.

She never knew when her uncle slipped back in the room and resumed his watch at her bed.

The mist in which Tara was standing kept moving, like clouds being shifted by a breeze, but every now and then the mist would part and she would get brief glimpses of a place she'd never seen before. It was gray and barren. The ground on which she stood felt as unsteady as the constantly moving mist. The obvious absence of life was as frightening as if she'd been facing the most ferocious of animals.

Then all of a sudden the mist in front of her began to dissipate, and in the distance, she saw Flynn standing on a rise. He kept turning in a circle, as if trying to get his bearings, and the look on his face was one of panic.

"Flynn! Flynn! Here! I'm here."

She saw him stop, and then turn toward the sound of her voice.

"I can't see you," he yelled.

"I'm here! Follow the sound of my voice."

He took a step forward and then stopped again as another voice came out of the mist.

"No, Flynn! This way. Come this way!"

Tara frowned. Who was that?

"Here, Flynn. I'm here," she yelled.

"No, Flynn. Come this way. Come to me."

Flynn put his hands over his ears. "Stop, stop. I don't know what to do. I don't know which way to go."

The mist shifted again and Flynn disappeared, but this time revealing his father a distance away.

Tara's heart skipped a beat. She should have known.

All of a sudden Michael was standing before her—glaring at her and angry by her presence.

"You don't belong here," he said. "Back off. Go away."

"Flynn doesn't belong here either, and yet you've called him to you and now he's lost. He needs to go back. He can't wake up until he does."

"No! I need him to come to me. There are things I need to tell him."

"You should have thought of that before you began using and selling

drugs. You should have thought of that while you were still alive. He would have visited you in prison any time and you know it."

"I didn't want him to see me in jail."

Tara was angry. "But you want him here? You'd will him to die to get what you want? What kind of a father are you?"

Suddenly O'Mara's anger was gone. He seemed unsure. "I don't want him to die."

"Then let him go. Let him get well, then I'll be the go-between for the both of you. I'll tell him everything you want him to hear. I'll be your voice."

Instead of an answer, O'Mara took a step back and was swallowed up by the mist.

Tara was scared. She didn't know what O'Mara was going to do next, but she couldn't leave without telling Flynn how to come back.

"Come back, Flynn! Please, come back. Listen for your mother's voice. Listen for mine. Follow the love, Flynn. Follow the love."

Chapter Eight

Two days later, Tara was released from the hospital, but the drive home was nerve-wracking. Every time they met a car she grew tense, and when the cars in front of them began slowing down for red lights, she grabbed hold of the door with one hand and her seat belt with the other.

Pat knew she was upset, but there was nothing he could do to make the ride any easier, except to keep reassuring her.

"It's okay, honey. I'm being careful and so are they. No one is speeding. No one is driving erratically, see?"

Tara nodded, but her heart was pounding so hard she could barely think. She kept expecting someone to hit them, or to ram the car from behind, and wondered if this fear would ever pass.

He decided to change the subject. "I got a phone call from the police last night. They want to get your statement about the accident. Apparently the driver of the sports car is claiming it was the truck driver's fault because something fell off the truck and caused him to swerve. He's denying all claims that any of it was his responsibility."

Tara was immediately angry, which was what he intended. "That's just crazy," she said. "He was speeding. He tried to pass that truck on the bridge, then whipped back into the lane behind the truck and clipped it. He hit the truck. He caused the trash to fall off and he's the one who hit us. Twice. "

"Glad you remember that," Pat said. "He knows Flynn is unconscious, and I think he was hoping you would have no memory of the accident."

"I remember everything, right up to the moment when I felt the water going over our heads."

"Lord have mercy," Pat said, his voice shaking.

"I'll tell them all of it. When is this happening?"

"I told them I'd call when we got home and set up a time."

"Is the creep still in jail?"

"I think so, although you know he'll make bail."

"But he almost killed us."

"That's how the law works. However, you just tell the police what you saw. They'll do the rest."

Tara nodded, but the anger she was feeling overshadowed her fear of traffic and before she knew it, they were home. Pat pulled up into the drive and then parked.

"Welcome home, baby girl."

Tara blinked. "We're here."

"Hold on a sec and I'll help you out."

She was grateful to be getting out of the car, and then noticed the back of the car was full of flowers.

"What about all those?"

"I'll bring them in after I get you inside."

Tara waited as he circled the car. When he opened the door, she stepped out. There were so many bruises appearing on her body that she looked like she'd been in a fight. Her legs still felt a little shaky and her chest hurt if she took too deep a breath. She was thankful for his support as they went inside.

"I never appreciated how good it is to be home," Tara said, and then immediately felt guilty that she was home and Flynn wasn't.

"Do you want to go to your room, or settle in here on the sofa?" Pat asked.

"The sofa, please. I've just spent the past two days in a bed. You can put my stuff in my bedroom, and be careful of my dream-catcher, Uncle Pat. Would you put a nail in the wall just over the headboard of my bed? I want to hang it there so I can see it when I lay down."

"I sure will. You settle in while I carry in the rest of the stuff, then I'll see about making us some lunch."

Tara sat down, but she couldn't stay there. As soon as Pat began bringing in the flowers, she started moving them all over the house, leaving some in the living room, a couple of the potted plants in the kitchen, and a small pot of violets in her bedroom. She took the asparagus fern into the bathroom, knowing that the moisture from their baths and showers would be good for it.

She'd never had flowers before, and now the house was full of them. It was a shame she'd had to drown for it happen. The good part was that she got to come back to this crazy world in which she lived. If only Flynn came back whole and healthy, she'd never ask God for another thing as long as she lived.

"Did you call the police?" Tara asked, as Pat came in with the last of her things.

"Yes. I told them we'd come down after lunch."

"Good. I'm going to get a cold pop."

"I'll get it, honey. Sit down and take it easy."

Tara sat, but she couldn't quit fidgeting. She couldn't get that dream about Flynn out of her head. She hadn't had it again, but it still gave her the creeps.

It wasn't a dream.

Tara moaned. "No. You mean that's really happening?"

He's lost.

Tara panicked. "Can you make O'Mara come see me again?"

He's like Flynn, caught in between. Neither here or there. I cannot communicate.

Tara felt sick.

"Here's your pop, honey. I poured it over ice."

Tara took the can and made herself shift focus. There were things that she needed to think about.

"Thanks, Uncle Pat." She took a sip of the cold Pepsi and then set it on the coffee table.

"I'm going to see what's in the fridge," Pat said.

"I won't want much. The thought of food makes me queasy."

"Okay. Hang tight. I won't be long," Pat said, and patted the top of her head just like he'd done when she was little.

The gesture was touching but she quickly blinked back the tears. She was done crying. It was time to declare war – war on the fool who'd nearly killed them, and war on a dead man who wouldn't let go of the son he'd left behind.

The police station was busy as Tara and her uncle walked in and approached the information desk.

"My niece is here to give a statement on the wreck she was in. The officer who's expecting us is named Blakely."

The man picked up the phone. "Have a seat. I'll tell him you're here."

They moved to a row of chairs against the wall and sat down.

A woman sitting nearby gave Pat a long, studied look. Tara saw her staring and frowned. When the woman realized Tara was watching her, she quickly looked away.

OMG. I can't believe that woman was thinking about hitting on my uncle.

Your Pat is a nice-looking man, Tara. I always thought he was a cutie pie—

Millicent! Do not finish that sentence and expect me to face you again.

Well, technically, Tara, you have never faced me, so I fail to see the point of that threat. However, I will desist.

Thank you.

Still, you have to admit that he's—

No! I don't want to hear this.

Tara heard a giggle, a pop, then saw a brief flash of pink smoke. Millicent was being outrageous today, dropping hints and not finishing them, talking about her uncle's sex appeal. Tara was so not in the mood.

At that point, a man came out of a hallway and called out her name. "Tara Luna?"

Tara and Pat stood up.

"I'm Officer Blakely. Follow me."

And just like that, everyone in the outer office did an about face as they recognized the name. She was the psychic who'd found people in the wreckage of the tornado—the same girl who'd been rescued from Boomer Lake.

Tara felt their gazes, and had to block out the random

thoughts from the room behind her as she and her uncle followed the officer back to his desk. He picked up a tape recorder, then led them to an interrogation room for privacy. After a few basic questions to establish her identity, the officer turned it over to Tara.

"Now, tell me, in your own words, exactly what happened and how the wreck occurred."

Tara began ticking off the incident, from the time they pulled out onto Lakeview Road to when they approached the bridge.

"He was driving way too fast and kept trying to pass the truck."

The officer stopped her. "Are you referring to the truck loaded with debris?"

"Yes. The truck and another car drove onto the bridge at the same time. They were both in the east-bound lanes of the bridge. You know that's a four-lane bridge, right? So the guy in the sports car tried to pass both the car *and* the truck, only there was traffic coming from the other direction. He slammed on his brakes and swerved back into the eastbound lane to keep from getting hit head-on. When he swerved back, he cut it too close. He missed the car, but hit the back-end of the truck. We saw him hit it. It was a really hard jolt and his car was already spinning out of control when the debris came loose."

Tara's hands were fisted in her lap, remembering the panic that she'd felt as she continued the story. "Flynn yelled at me to watch out, and was already braking when the debris hit the sports car, and then the car hit us. The driver hit us once on the front bumper, and when we started to spin, he hit us again on the rear bumper.

"That's when we went airborne over the railing and into the lake. I unbuckled our seat belts and was trying to get us out of the car, but Flynn kept saying he couldn't breathe, and then the water was over our heads." Tara stopped and took a deep breath to keep her voice from shaking. "It is that driver's fault that the accident occurred. His driving was reckless and too fast. He caused it all and I'll swear that on a stack of Bibles."

Officer Blakely turned off the tape recorder and stood up. "I'll have this typed up and then you can sign it, okay?"

Tara leaned back and closed her eyes as the officer left the room.

"You okay?" Pat asked. "I mean, this isn't too strenuous for you?"

"I'm mad, not weak."

Pat relaxed. Anger was healthy. It meant she was moving past the shock.

"Can we please go by the hospital before we go home? I still haven't seen Flynn."

He hesitated. "If you're sure you're up to it."

"I can't rest until I see him, Uncle Pat."

"Okay. I understand. But since he's in ICU, we may have to wait a bit for the next visiting time. They're very strict about it there."

"I don't care how long I wait. I have to talk to him."

Pat frowned. "But I thought you said he wasn't going to wake up for a while."

"He's not, but he will be able to hear me."

"Seriously?"

"Yes. Seriously."

A short while later Officer Blakely was back. He slid the statement in front of her.

"Please read that over to make sure there are no errors and then sign and date it."

Tara read it, signed it and then handed it back. Their hands touched, and in that moment she saw something about Blakely that he needed to know.

"Who's Shorty?"

Blakely blinked. His mouth dropped. "Uh . . ."

"Never mind. I don't need to know his identity, but you need to know whatever he's telling you is a lie. Don't invest your money. It's a scam."

Blakely already knew the girl's reputation, but he hadn't really believed it until now. "Shorty is my brother-in-law."

"Ouch," Tara said. "Sorry about that. Have you already

given him the check?"

"Holy Moses," Blakely muttered and took a step backward. "Uh . . . he's coming by tonight to pick it up."

Tara frowned. "I think there are others. Maybe a dozen people who've already invested in his scheme. Go to the Deeds and Records office. I think the land deed he showed you is a forgery. The land in question still belongs to someone else. He's going to take the money and run."

"Son-of-a-bitch," Blakely mumbled, then realized what he'd said. "Sorry, I shouldn't have said—"

"It's fine," Tara said. "I'm really sorry."

Blakely seemed to come to his senses and instead, shook Tara's hand.

"No, don't be sorry. Thank you. I had a bad feeling about this from the start, but it's my wife's brother and she was so certain it would be a good deal. What I need to do now is check out that deed like you said and go from there. Thanks kid, thanks a bunch. I haven't ever arrested a family member before, but I have a feeling it's about to happen."

"Yes, well, good luck," Tara said.

Blakely grinned. "I don't need luck. You already changed it for me by the warning. Come on, I'll walk you out of the precinct."

By the time they reached the car, Tara felt lighter just from being able to help him avert financial disaster.

Pat eyed Tara as she began to buckle up. "I'd like to be a fly on his wall tonight, wouldn't you?"

She shook her head. "Not me. It's going to hit the fan big time. He doesn't know it, but his wife is in on it. She has a gambling problem and her brother was going to give her that check for pay-off money to a loan shark. It will all come out in the wash, as they say."

"Oh lord," Pat said, and then grinned. "You are something. I wish your mother had lived to help you through all this. With me, you're just finding your way all alone."

"I'm not alone, Uncle Pat. I have you for the real stuff, and Millicent and Henry for the weird stuff. If I can just get Flynn to come back, it will all be good."

Pat frowned. "Come back? You mean, wake up?"

"Something like that. Now can we go to the hospital?"

"That we can."

There were more than a dozen students from their class in the ICU waiting room when Tara and Pat walked in. Tara stopped short, startled by their presence, but Mona jumped up and went to meet her.

"Sweetheart . . . oh Tara," she said, and gave her a gentle hug. "I can tell you were hurt. All those cuts and bruises . . . but I'm so glad you're okay. Seeing you walking in like this gives me hope for Flynn."

Despite her intent not to cry, Tara's eyes filled with tears. "He got hurt in the wreck before we even got in the water."

"But you helped save him. Pat said you unbuckled the both of you after the car was in the lake, and then held his head out of the water until . . . until . . ." Mona covered her face. "I'm sorry. It's all so horrible."

"Yes, ma'am. It is, but I need to talk to you privately, and to ask your permission if I can see Flynn when it's the next visiting time. I know they only allow one or two family members at a time, but it's really important."

Mona looked startled, then took Tara by the hand and led her out of the waiting room and into a small alcove down the hall.

"Talk to me," she said.

"You know what I can do, right? I mean, you're okay with it and everything?"

"Oh honey, I don't know how it works, but I have the utmost regard and respect of you."

Tara nodded. "Okay, then here's the deal. Flynn is still unconscious, right?"

Mona nodded as tears ran down her cheeks. "The doctor is calling it a coma."

Tara sighed. "Yes. But here's what you need to know. Flynn

isn't waking up because his spirit is not in his body. It was called out, and now he's lost and can't find his way back. When you're with him, you need to talk to him and tell him to follow the sound of your voice, and that it will all be okay. He just needs to come home."

Mona looked horrified. "How does stuff like that happen?"

"Your ex-husband did it. I saw him here yesterday. He followed Flynn into surgery and he's the one who called Flynn out. I saw them both in a dream. I tried to talk to Flynn but he couldn't see me. When he tried to follow my voice, O'Mara called him in the other direction. He doesn't want him to leave. I challenged O'Mara and he's mad at me, but I keep hoping he'll do the right thing and let Flynn go. Flynn is scared and confused, and the only way we can help him come back is to keep talking him home."

Mona was so mad she was shaking. "That is just like him—selfish to the core. He ruined our marriage, nearly ruined Flynn and I financially, and just when I think he's out of our lives, he won't die."

"Oh, he's dead, and he needs to cross over. I told him I'd gladly be the go-between for him and Flynn later, but Flynn needs to get well first."

"What did Mike say?"

"He just disappeared."

Mona clutched Tara's hand. "I'll talk to Flynn every moment I get, and yes, of course you can see him. Anytime you want."

"You can also weigh in and do some one-on-one talking to your ex-husband, as well. Maybe you'll have some influence with him. I sure don't," Tara said.

"It's going to be another thirty minutes before visitation. Let's go back into the waiting room. You need to sit down," Mona said. "Your fellow students have been so sweet coming and going, bringing me food and clean clothes from my house . . . even saying prayers with me. I never knew he had so many friends."

"Bad times either bring out the best or the worst of

people," Tara said.

"They've been asking about you, too. They didn't know you'd already checked out when they arrived, so they'll be glad to talk to you."

Tara followed Mona back to the waiting room and was quickly pulled into the group, fielding hugs and well-wishes. It made her feel strong with all the friendship at her back.

When the time finally came for visitors to go into ICU, Tara was on her feet and trying not to panic. She didn't know what to expect and wasn't ready to face seeing Flynn hooked up to a half-dozen machines that were keeping him alive.

"You go alone this time," Mona said, and pushed Tara forward. "Do your thing, honey."

Tara took a deep breath and went into ICU like she was going to war, with her head up and her eyes flashing. She followed Mona's direction past the other patients and straight to his bed. Other than oxygen and a heart monitor, Flynn looked the same. But he was so still. If it hadn't been for the repetitive beep of the heart monitor she would have thought he was dead.

There was a moment when she felt like she was coming undone, and then she remembered what she'd come here to do. She took his hand and then leaned over and began talking to him in a low, quiet voice.

"Hey you, it's me, Tara. I know you're lost, but you saw me didn't you, and I know you can hear me now. You need to come back so you can get well. You want to get well, don't you?" Tara's voice started to shake. "I want you to get well. I heart you very much, remember? I know you're lost, but when you hear your mother or me talking to you, follow the love, Flynn. We're trying to help you come home."

She watched his face, praying for a sign that he could hear her, but he didn't even flinch. She tried not to let it get her down.

"That's okay. I know you're in there. Just come back to us. Please. Don't listen to your Dad. I'll help the both of you later. Trust me on this. Come back. Please, come back."

Tara wrapped her hand around his wrist and closed her eyes, trying to key in on that part of Flynn that made him real, but it didn't happen. Still, she wasn't about to give up.

"Look for me tonight," she whispered. "I'll try to find you again in my dreams, okay? We'll come back together."

And just like that, the visiting time was over.

"I have to go now, but I'll be back. I won't let you go, Flynn. I promise. I'll find a way to get you home."

She left ICU with a knot in her belly, but she wasn't about to give up.

Mona was waiting for her when she came out. "Did you talk to him? Did you tell him to come home?"

"Yes, and when you go in again, you do the same. I told him to follow the love. He'll be listening for the sound of your voice."

Mona pressed a hand against her belly. "This is a nightmare."

"I agree," Tara said.

"Pat's in the waiting room. Follow me," Mona said.

Tara was right on her heels as they headed back to the waiting room. As they stepped aside to let a nurse pushing a food cart pass, Tara caught movement from the corner of her eye. When she turned to look, she saw the backside of a red-headed woman disappear around the corner. It made her remember the weird redhead who'd tried to come into her room, but when they got back to the waiting room, she promptly forgot about it.

As they walked into the room, even more kids from their class had arrived. Bethany Fanning and her boyfriend, Davis Breedlove, were sitting on the floor against the wall, talking to Nikki and Corey. When they saw Tara they quickly got up.

"This is awful," Bethany said. "We're so sorry this happened to you guys, and while Flynn has a ways to go to get better, we're so grateful you're okay."

"Hey, I came out of it, remember? Flynn will, too," Corey said.

"I remember, and I'm counting on it," Tara said.

Mac and Penny walked in and when they saw Tara, they both began to cry.

"We're so sorry," Mac said, as she gave Tara a hug.

"Everyone is meeting at the gym tonight for a candlelight vigil," Penny said. "We tried to call you to let you know, but you didn't pick up."

Tara sighed. "That's because my phone is at the bottom of Boomer Lake."

They looked stunned. "OMG . . . we didn't think."

Pat moved into the conversation. He was getting concerned about Tara. She was pale and slightly stooped. He knew her chest and ribs were still sore from when they'd done CPR. He wanted her home and in bed, resting.

"Tara?"

Tara saw the worry on her uncle's face. "I'm okay, but I *am* ready to go home."

"Will we see you at the vigil?" Mac asked.

"No, she'll be home and in bed," Pat said.

"He's right," Tara said. "I'm about out of steam, but thank you . . . all of you. Flynn will be so grateful when he finds out what a great job you're doing taking care of his mom."

"If you need anything, call me," Nikki said.

"Thanks," Tara said, waved at the kids from her school, then left with her uncle's arm across her shoulder.

Pat eyed her closely as they got on the elevator. "You're exhausted, aren't you?"

She nodded.

"Bed. As soon as I get you home."

"I won't argue."

They drove home in silence, both of them lost in thought.

Once when they stopped for a red light, Tara thought she caught a glimpse of a man on a motorcycle a couple of cars behind them, but then forgot about it. Motorcycles were everywhere. It didn't mean it was the guy who'd pulled them out of the lake.

When they got home, Tara paused before going to her room.

"Uncle Pat, you need to go back to work tomorrow, okay? I'm fine and we can't afford to lose the pay."

"I don't know. I hate to—"

"No. I promise I'm perfectly capable of taking care of myself."

He hesitated then finally agreed. "I'll call in."

As soon as he sat down to make the call, Tara went to her bedroom. The dream-catcher was lying on her bed and Pat had done as she'd asked and put a nail in the wall above her bed. She picked it up and slipped the cord over the nail, tilted it until it was hanging level, then stood back to see how it looked.

The feathers shifted, as if a breeze was blowing through the room, but the windows were shut. Tara's eyes narrowed. It wasn't Millicent or Henry. They didn't sneak around when they came through.

"Who's here?" she called. "O'Mara, is that you?"

The room stayed quiet and no spirits materialized, leaving Tara unsettled, and without answers. Disgusted with the ghost's stubborn behavior, but at a loss as to how to stop him, she crawled into bed, covered up with a blanket, and closed her eyes.

The phone rang intermittently, but she ignored it. When she heard someone knocking on the front door, she was glad Uncle Pat was here to run interference. She knew hiding wasn't going to change anything, but she needed this time to regroup.

You know who pulled you out of the car.

And just like that, Tara was wide awake. She sat straight up in bed.

"What do you mean, I know who it is?"

You know him.

"How do I know him? What's his name? Why did he leave?"

To Tara's disgust, Millicent had nothing more to say. It was days like this that made her crazy. She got out of bed, changed into her oldest pair of jeans, her favorite sweatshirt, put on socks and her house shoes and headed for the kitchen.

Pat followed her. "What are you doing?"

"I'm looking to see what we have to make for supper."

"You're not cooking. We can go out, or I'll pick something up and bring home."

"I can't go out and you know it. People will be weird."

"Then I'll have something delivered. What are you hungry for?"

She thought a moment. "Pancakes. I could eat pancakes."

Pat grinned. "That's easy, but I will make them. You rest. I'll call you when they're done."

"Do we have syrup? If we don't, we can make syrup like you used to, remember?"

Pat's smile widened. "Yeah, I remember. Poor man's pancake syrup, right? Equal parts of brown sugar and water, heat to a boil, and stir until the sugar is dissolved."

"I like that syrup even better than what we buy," Tara said.

Pat laughed. "That's because it's all we ever had for years. Want me to make some tonight?"

She nodded.

"It's a deal," he said. "Now, either take yourself back to bed or use the living room sofa. Take your pick."

"Sofa. Maybe I can sleep after we eat."

She went back to the living room, dug the remote out from between the sofa cushions and turned on the TV while Uncle Pat began banging skillets and cabinet doors. The programming was mind-numbing as she stared blankly at the screen. But she didn't see the shows. She saw Flynn, lying in that hospital bed, dead to this world and lost in another.

It began to rain just before dark. At the first rumble of thunder, Tara bolted out onto the back porch and looked up at the sky, scared it was going to storm.

Pat followed her out. "What's wrong, honey?"

"Is there going to be another tornado?"

"No. I just listened to the weather report. It's just a thunder storm. Not a bit of bad weather predicted anywhere in the state, okay?"

"You're sure?"

"I'm very sure."

She sat down in a chair beneath the covered porch and let

herself relax as Pat went back inside. She'd always enjoyed rainy days, and falling asleep to the sound of rain on the roof used to be a good thing. It was going to take some time to get back to that mind-set again.

I once made love with a count inside a carriage with the rain blowing in the windows.

Tara rolled her eyes. "OMG, Millicent. I do not need to know this."

My boop.

Tara grinned. "If you meant to say *my bad*, then yes, it definitely is."

I have to say, the rain did dampen his ardor.

Tara laughed out loud, and then the moment she did, was shocked that it happened.

Laughter heals. It is a good thing.

Tara sighed. "I don't know what I'd do without you and Henry, but I sure wish you could run interference for me with Flynn. If you know a magic word or two on how to send Michael O'Mara into the light, let me know."

It is his choice alone.

Tara sighed. "I was afraid you'd say that."

A gust of wind blew rain beneath the porch and onto Tara's bare arms and feet.

"Brr, that's cold," she said, and got up and went inside.

The kitchen still smelled like pancakes, but the dishes were done. She could hear the television in the living room, which meant Uncle Pat was settled in for the night. Tomorrow was Friday, but there was still no school, which in one way was a blessing.

She felt unsettled and naked. Her deepest secrets had been revealed to the public in the most blatant of ways. Her psychic abilities had always been hers to tell when the need arose, not broadcast willy-nilly to whoever happened to be watching TV. And yet with all those seemingly magic skills, they were useless to help her sweet Flynn.

Her shoulders slumped. Standing alone in the middle of the kitchen, she closed her eyes and bowed her head.

"Please God, help me to help Flynn."

Thunder rumbled overhead, rattling the windows.

Tara lifted her head. She sure hoped that meant she'd been heard. Now all she had to do was pay attention.

She went back to her bedroom to lie down. The last thing she remembered looking at was her dream-catcher before sleep finally took her under.

The mist was thicker than before, but the ground was moving beneath Tara's feet. She kept trying to keep her balance, but for every step she took forward, the ground rolled her back two steps, as if trying to throw her back to where she'd come from.

Only she'd come for a reason and wasn't leaving until she'd accomplished it. She began calling Flynn's name, determined to reconnect. As she did, the mist began to encircle her, wrapping her into a vortex and trapping the sound of her voice inside. She knew immediately that was O'Mara's work. He knew she was here and was trying to block her from Flynn. She felt helpless and angry, and began screaming taunts, trying to make O'Mara come to her.

"You're a coward, Michael O'Mara! You're an unnatural father, putting your only child in danger and then hiding behind this weak excuse for precipitation. What kind of a man does this? As for this stunt you just pulled, it's nothing. It can't hurt me. You can't scare me. But you're killing your son. Let him go! For the love of God, let him go!"

The vortex stopped as suddenly as it had begun and Michael O'Mara was standing before her, but this time he wasn't alone. Without speaking, he put Flynn's hand in hers and disappeared.

Flynn looked at Tara, almost as if she was a stranger.

"It's me," Tara said. "It's Tara. Come with me and I'll show you the way home."

"Home?"

"Do you remember home?"

He shook his head.

"Do you remember me?"

He looked like he was going to cry.

Tara's heart sank. He'd been in here too long. This didn't bode well for what he'd be like when he woke up—if he woke up.

"It's okay, Flynn. I'll remember for you. Come with me. I know the way back."

Chapter Nine

"Tara, Tara, wake up, honey."

Tara gasped as she opened her eyes. Her uncle was standing over her bed, still in his old tie-dye pajamas.

"Uncle Pat? What's wrong?"

"You were screaming, honey. It must have been a bad dream."

Tara sat up in bed and shoved the hair away from her face.

"Screaming? What was I saying?"

"You kept crying, 'Say my name, say my name.'"

All of a sudden Tara remembered. She glanced up at the dream-catcher hanging over her bed as her shoulders slumped.

"Oh, yeah. Now I remember."

"Are you going to be okay?" Pat asked.

"Yes. I'm sorry I woke you."

"It's almost time to get up anyway. Are you sure you're going to be okay on your own here today?"

"I'll be fine, Uncle Pat. I swear. I won't go anywhere. I don't need anything except rest."

He smiled. "Okay then. So, how about I take you out for supper after I get home from work, and then we'll go by the hospital so you can see Flynn again?"

"Yes on seeing Flynn, again, but not sure if I'm ready to face another onslaught of people wanting their fortunes told," she muttered.

Pat frowned. "Well you're damn sure not going to hide in this house for the rest of your life. We're going to go about our business, and if anyone meddles in it, then we'll send them packing. Okay?"

Tara sighed. He made it sound so simple. If only that was the case.

"I'm going to make some scrambled eggs. Would you like some, too? You can always go back to bed when I'm gone, and at least I'll know you had one good meal before I left."

"Scrambled eggs sound good," Tara said.

"Give me about fifteen minutes and then come and get it," he said.

Tara waited until she heard him leave the bathroom across the hall and then she got up and went to wash her face and brush her hair. She grabbed a hair band, put her hair back in a ponytail and then returned to her room to dress. Fall of the year was closing in and the mornings were cooler. She dug a pair of house shoes from the back of the closet and slipped them on, then stopped in front of the mirror over her dresser.

She still looked the same—a too-tall girl with long dark hair. She used to fool herself by thinking if she squinted her eyes just right, she almost looked like Angelina Jolie. But she didn't see that today. All she saw was a girl with a bruised and battered face and an out-of-control life.

Before the tornado, it had seemed as if time was standing still. Being a high school senior was like standing on the edge of a high diving board without being allowed to jump into the pool. They were waiting for the time when they'd be out on their own, finding out what growing up and being an adult was all about. So many devastating things had happened since the storm Tara felt like time had taken wing, and the faster it went, the farther it was taking her from Flynn.

"Breakfast is ready!" Pat yelled.

Tara stuck her tongue out at herself and headed for the kitchen.

But Tara didn't go back to bed when her uncle left for work. She put a load of clothes in to wash and then got her iPod and stretched out on the sofa to listen to some tunes. When the washer stopped, she put the load into the dryer and then stopped in the kitchen to get a cold can of Pepsi before going back into the living room.

She glanced at the clock as she sat back down, marking the time so she'd know when to check on the dryer. She was shuffling through her playlist for something upbeat and missed seeing a van pulling up at the curb in front of the house.

Henry popped up at the end of the sofa and started waving his arms and pointing toward the door. Tara took the ear-buds out of her ears and laid the iPod on the coffee table. She was about to go see what had stirred him up when she heard a knock at the door.

Ah. That explained the warning. She peered through the curtain, saw the logo on the side of the van and knew it was from a Tulsa television station. How had they found where she lived?

They knocked again, only louder and longer.

Tara hesitated. She'd told Uncle Pat she'd be fine, but she hadn't counted on the media running her down.

We've got this.

Tara hesitated. "I think I should call someone . . . maybe the police?"

Au contraire, mon cher.

Tara rolled her eyes. Usually, when Millicent began speaking French, weird things happened. She peered through the curtains again, careful not to let the news crew see her, and recognized the woman from late-night news casts. The camera the man was carrying gave away his reason for being there.

Just as they were about to knock again, a huge flock of blackbirds suddenly appeared out of nowhere, flew across the yard, and swooped under the porch roof. Between the cacophony of chirps and squawks, and the random unloading of bird poop, the pair on the porch never had a chance to duck.

The man began swinging the camera and cursing in intermittent bursts and shrieks as he jumped off the porch and made a run for the van.

The woman's scream was a high octave E Flat as she tore down the steps, waving her arms and pulling birds out of her hair as she went. She jumped into the van and then slammed the door behind her.

Tara watched as the driver took off, laying rubber halfway

down the block, with the flock of birds following them, dive-bombing the windshield and the side windows as they sped away. She could only imagine what they must be thinking, but she doubted they would be back.

Confident that her troubles were over, she went back to the sofa.

"Thanks guys," she said, as she picked up her iPod.

No problemo.

Tara laughed. "So we've moved from French to fake Spanish?"

I aim to please. Ta Ta, toots.

Tara was still smiling when she went to get her clean clothes out of the dryer and hang them up.

French Langdon witnessed the incident from his hiding place across the street. Although he wasn't sure what he'd seen, he was beginning to believe everything he'd heard about Tara Luna might have been understated. The thing with the birds was straight out of a horror movie. Still, he had his orders to keep an eye on her. She was no good to any of them dead, and all he needed to do was make sure she stayed in one piece.

It was after 12:00 p.m. before Tara finally sat down to eat, but then the soup was too hot. She was blowing and stirring it, waiting for it to cool when the phone began to ring. When she saw it was from Mona, she panicked and made a quick grab.

"Hello? Mona? Is everything all right?"

"Oh, yes, honey. I'm sorry I scared you. It's actually good news. The doctor just told me that Flynn is beginning to show signs of coming around."

Tara was so relieved that she jumped out of the chair and began to pace as she talked.

"Oh! Oh wow, that is great, so great! Is he moving . . . talking . . . anything like that?"

"I don't think so. Not just yet. But the doctor said his vital signs are changing. His heart rate is getting better and his blood pressure isn't as low. He said that when they shine a light in his eye, the pupil contracts. These are all positive responses."

"OMG, I've so been hoping this would happen. Thank you so much for letting me know."

"You had a hand in this, didn't you?"

"We all did. Is it okay if I come by again this evening to see him?"

"Of course."

Tara hesitated. She didn't want to be nosey, but she knew Flynn and his mom lived from paycheck to paycheck like they did.

"Are you okay? I mean . . . are they giving you a hard time at Eskimo Joe's about coming back to work?"

"No. They're being wonderful. They even put up donation jars all over Joe's to help with the hospital bills."

"You aren't going to have to pay those bills, Mona. The creep who caused the wreck is gonna be stuck with all that and then some. Talk to Uncle Pat. He can fill you in on what's been happening."

"I'll talk to him this evening while you're visiting Flynn. So, I'll see you later then?"

"Yes, definitely, and thank you so much for calling me. This is the best news ever."

"You're welcome, honey. You're the best thing that's ever happened to Flynn. I hope you know that."

Tara was dumbfounded. She stammered something she hoped was appropriate before Mona hung up, and knew she was blushing because her cheeks were hot.

OMG. The best thing? Seriously?

Alert! Alert!

Tara jumped. "Alert on what? What's happening? Is someone else outside?"

It's the cops!

Tara glanced at her rapidly cooling soup and then went back to the living room to check the front yard. Sure enough a car was pulling up into the drive, but when she saw who was getting out, she relaxed.

"Ease up, Millicent. It's our two fave detectives."

Rutherford is cute.

"No bird attacks, and I'm meeting them on the porch, so no interference. Okay?"

Not unless they overstep their bounds.

Tara rolled her eyes. "Seriously, Millicent. They're cops. They have the right to overstep bounds and stuff."

Not with you, they don't.

"Yes, well, there's that. Just let me handle this, okay?"

My lips are sealed.

Tara snorted lightly as she headed for the door, unwilling to invite them in. She was still miffed at them for trying to trick her into saying something that would incriminate Flynn in Floy Nettles' murder.

Tara waited until they were about to come up the steps and then opened the door. Both men stopped in mid-step, obviously surprised by her sudden appearance as she stepped out on the porch, closing the door behind her.

Rutherford noticed it. So she wasn't inviting them in. He guessed he understood. She'd had one hell of a week, and from what he'd heard about her boyfriend, hell wasn't over yet.

Detective Allen smiled. He wanted on the good side of this girl so her crazy ghosts wouldn't screw with them again.

"Hi, Tara. It sure is good to see you up and about."

Rutherford decided to follow his partner's lead. "Yeah, kid. You been through hell . . . excuse my language . . . haven't you?"

Tara folded her arms across her chest and leaned against a porch post. "What's up?" she said.

"Uh, we had a report that there was a disturbance at your house, and since you're one of our favorite people, we told the patrol unit that we'd check it out for them. We wanted to make sure you were okay."

Tara frowned. "Disturbance? What kind of disturbance?"

Rutherford checked his notebook. "Uh, well, the report that came in said a news crew was run off of this property by a flock of birds."

Tara arched an eyebrow. "Birds? Seriously? And how does

any of that concern me?"

Allen scratched his head. "Uh, well, you know . . . we figured maybe those spooks of yours might have had something to do with it."

"Oooh, I so would not refer to Millicent as a spook."

"Sorry, really sorry," Detective Allen looked nervous, and then took a step backward and glanced toward the sky, then at the trees, just in case.

Rutherford wasn't as easily put off. "I'm guessing a news crew arrived unannounced and made a pest of themselves."

Tara shrugged. "I never talked to them. I heard a knock at the door. By the time I got to the living room, they were already off the porch, screaming their heads off and running for the van. Scared me, I can tell you. I didn't know what was happening."

Rutherford eyed the bland expression on her face and then frowned. "So, that's your story."

She didn't blink. "Anything else I can do for you?"

He sighed. "Look kid. We haven't had a chance to talk to you since the tornado, and then the wreck you were in. It's been pretty crazy in Stillwater, but, I want you to know how proud we were of your efforts during search and rescue, and how thankful we are that you got out of that wreck alive."

"Thank you."

"You're still pretty bruised up. All of that is going to heal, right?"

"Yes. I'm pretty sore from the wreck and then the CPR, but nothing was broken."

"Uh, we heard your boyfriend wasn't so lucky. Is he getting better?"

"It appears he might be making a turn for the better, although he has yet to wake up. He's in a coma."

"That's rough. We're all pulling for him, too. You can tell him that when you talk to him next."

"I will. Have you arrested anyone yet for Floy Nettles' murder?"

Rutherford shook his head. "We're still following up on leads."

"Which means you don't have a clue, right?" Tara said.

Allen frowned. "We're not at liberty to discuss police business with citizens."

Suddenly Tara flashed on a picture of a woman and two men standing on the edge of a lake drinking beer. One man was Michael O'Mara, the other was Sam Nettles. Without question, Tara knew the woman was with Sam.

"Uh, what did Sam Nettles' wife have to say about all that's happened?"

Rutherford's eyes widened. "Sam Nettles doesn't have a wife."

Tara could see her plain as she was seeing the men standing before her.

"He might not be married, but there was a woman in his life when O'Mara was running with them, which means there *is* one other person who could have known about all that money, and you don't have all the possible suspects in jail after all. You should check that out."

"Well hell . . . excuse my language," Rutherford muttered. "How did we miss that?"

Tara shrugged. "If it hadn't been for the tornado hitting town and shifting everyone's focus, you would probably have picked up on it sooner or later."

Allen's ears were red, which meant he didn't like being caught out with sloppy detective work, but Rutherford was inclined to agree with her.

"So, I guess the mystery of the random bird attack will have to remain a mystery," he said.

Tara agreed. "Surely there's no way to predict what wild things will do. Something probably spooked them, and that reporter and her cameraman just got caught in their path."

"Yeah, that sounds about right. At any rate, that's what's going in the report, and thanks for the heads up about the wife bit. You have a nice day, okay?"

"You too," Tara said, and then stood on the porch and watched them leave. As they drove out of sight, she caught a glimpse of someone watching her from across the street.

Something about the way he was standing struck a familiar chord. After all that she'd recently endured, the thought of some peeping Tom hanging around the neighborhood ticked her off. She put her hands on her hips and defiantly stared back.

French Langdon became so caught up in watching the Luna chick talking to the cops that before he knew it, he was caught. The moment he knew she'd made him, instead of running, he decided to wait her out to see what she did. After all, he had a pretty good cover story. They were in school together and lived in the same town. It could happen.

But when she stared back at him in defiance, he had to stifle a grin. She was something, this girl. If things had been different, he would have considered giving that O'Mara kid a run for his money. She was the kind of woman a guy could get serious about, although she was a little young for him. Still, he was a patient man and time would take care of the age thing.

He crossed his arms across his chest.

She flipped him off and went back in the house.

He laughed out loud and then made himself scarce.

Tara was furious. She'd figured out who it was and didn't know what to make of it. Why would that new guy, French Langdon, be spying on her? Was he trying to get up the nerve to come ask her some dumb ass question about his future, or was it something more sinister? He wasn't the most clean-cut guy in town. No telling what he was mixed up in. But whatever it was, it better not have anything to do with her. She was fed up to the gills with mercenary people.

He rides a Harley.

Tara spun. "No! Are you serious?"

Did that sound like a joke? I apologize. I did not mean to speak lightly.

"That's not what I meant and you know it," Tara said, as she dashed back to the window and looked out, but he was gone. "Are you saying that the new guy at school is the one who pulled Flynn and me out of the lake? Is he really the one who saved us?"

He knows how to swim, and he is not all that he appears to be.

"Millicent, damn it! Just once could I have a direct answer instead of a riddle?"

If you want answers, then you need to ask the right questions of the proper person, and for the record, cursing is unladylike.

Tara groaned. "What are you saying?"

Ask him yourself when you see him at school.

Tara was muttering to herself as she rechecked the door to make sure it was locked, and then plopped down on the sofa and turned on the TV. Henry materialized feet first on the sofa beside her, then blew her a kiss which was his standard greeting.

Tara sighed. "I love you, too . . . both of you, and you know it. I don't mean to sound unappreciative."

He shook his head and smiled as he patted his chest, which meant he loved her, too.

She pulled her knees up beneath her chin and stared pensively out the window.

"I'm just so worried about Flynn and fed up with all this crazy, unexpected attention that I got short with the both of you and I'm sorry, okay?"

He nodded.

Okay.

"Thanks guys. So I feel like taking a nap. Will you give me a warning wake-up if the need arises?"

Absolutely.

Henry gave her a thumbs up.

Tara turned the sound down so that it was little more than a murmur, then stretched out on the sofa, pulled the afghan over her legs and closed her eyes. Minutes later, she was sound asleep.

She slept without moving for almost two hours and when she woke, the first thing she thought of was Nikki. Today was her birthday and she hadn't gotten her a gift.

OMG. What kind of a BFF was she to forget something like that?

You were hardly in the shape to go shopping, although I do love it when you try on pretty things. You'd look good in something red and slinky.

"Seriously, Millicent? Red and slinky? I wear blue jeans and tees, not red silk."

Tara's sore muscles protested as she got up from the sofa. She moved gingerly toward the bathroom, and when she came out, she was still wrestling with the issue of gifts. She went to the kitchen, grabbed a cookie and the rest of the pop she hadn't finished this morning, and then called Nikki. The least she could do was wish her happy birthday.

The phone rang several times and just when she thought it was going to voice mail, Nikki picked up.

"Hi, Tara. How are you feeling?"

"Oh, I'm still sore. I just called to wish you a happy birthday. I haven't had a chance to get you a gift yet."

"Oh, no gifts. Did you forget? With all that's happened since I issued the invitation, it's no wonder. There were to be no gifts. The slumber party with my BFFS was my present. And, you aren't the only one who's sick now. Mac called me earlier. She's throwing up. Caught something from her little brother, probably."

"Ugh. Poor Mac," Tara said. "Are you doing something fun today anyway? You should. You only turn eighteen once, you know."

"Daddy made me waffles for breakfast, which I love, and Mom took me to get my nails done. The sisters are bugging me, as usual, but it's all a good day. I wish you were here? If you felt like it, we could come get you."

"Thanks, but I'm not much fun right now. Oh! My gosh, I can't believe I didn't tell you this first. Mona called me this morning. The doctors think Flynn is coming out of the coma. All his vital signs are getting better."

Nikki squealed, and then yelled out the news to her family, before getting back on the line. "Now that is a great birthday present. I'll let Mac and Penny know."

"Okay."

"Uh, hey . . . I have a question. What do you know about

French Langdon?" Tara asked.

"Who?" Nikki said.

"You know, the Dracula guy."

"Oh! Him! I don't know anything, why?"

Tara kept pushing. "One of the teachers mentioned he was a transfer. Do you know anything about him?"

"Nope! I'd never seen him before the day we were talking about him in the cafeteria. Why?"

Tara's eyes narrowed. He was still a mystery, and she'd had all of the drama she could stomach for a while. "No reason. I just saw him today and wondered about him, that's all."

"He's weird, that's for sure," Nikki said. "And for some reason, he seems way older than us, but that's just me."

Tara frowned. Now that Nikki mentioned it, the guy did stick out like a sore thumb among the other boys at school. What she thought strange was that she hadn't picked up on any of this on her own.

"Okay . . . enough about the weird guy. Happy birthday. See you Monday at school."

"Absolutely," Nikki said. "Talk to you later."

Tara hung up, and then carried her cookie and pop into the living room just as another car pulled into their driveway. Only this time it was just the landlord, Mr. Whiteside.

Tara went outside to meet him. "Hi, Mr. Whiteside."

"Oh. I didn't think about you being home, but I should have. There's still no school, is there?"

"No sir, not until Monday."

"I've been keeping up with you through the news. You are certainly blessed to have survived that terrible wreck. How's your friend?"

"They think he's getting better."

"Good, good. Listen, I planned on removing the rest of these fallen limbs today, but the chainsaw is pretty noisy. Were you resting?"

"I just woke up from a nap, so your timing is great,' Tara said. "Go right ahead."

He smiled and waved and then started the chainsaw.

Tara grimaced at the roar and went back inside. Even with the door closed she could still hear the noise, so she just turned up the volume on the TV and settled in to watch a movie.

A short while later, she happened to glance up at the clock and realized her uncle would be coming home soon. He'd promised to take her out to supper tonight and she wasn't even dressed.

She went to her room and began sorting through clothes, trying to figure out what she wanted to wear. Her body was still too sore for anything that wasn't soft and comfy. After deciding on a pair of jeans and a long-sleeved sweatshirt, she changed, then went to the bathroom to put on makeup and fix her hair.

The bathroom had no window and the overhead light wasn't as bright as the rest of the house, but it still highlighted the dark bruises on Tara's neck and face. A couple of them were beginning to turn a slight shade of purple and green, which meant they were healing, but it did nothing for her self-esteem. Between her reputation and her appearance, she was a walking advertisement for disaster. She sure hoped Uncle Pat knew what he was doing by taking her out tonight. It could turn into an embarrassing mess.

Mr. Whiteside was still there loading up limbs when Uncle Pat came home. Tara saw him drive in, then stop to talk to their landlord before coming inside. The closer the time came to go visit Flynn, the more anxious she'd become. She'd already laid out clean clothes for Pat. All he had to do was shower and change and they'd be off.

A couple of minutes later, he came inside.

"Hey, honey. You look all pretty and rested. Was the day too boring being here alone?"

Tara grinned. Between the news crew, the bird attack, the detectives checking out a complaint, her run-in with Dracula, and Mr. Whiteside's chainsaw, it had been anything but boring.

"It was fine. I laid out your clean clothes. All you need to do is clean up and we're good to go."

Pat kissed her cheek as he sailed past. "You are a sweetheart. I won't be long."

He paused halfway down the hall and yelled back. "Hey, did you decide where you wanted to go eat?"

"Except for the Hideaway Pizza, I don't know which places have opened back up since the tornado."

"Oh, well, then I'll think on it while I'm showering and then you can pick from the ones I know about, okay?"

She nodded, but the truth was she didn't much care. Food still wasn't the priority it had been. It hadn't occurred to her that she was associating the thought of food with what had happened to her and Flynn, because they'd been on their way to Texas Roadhouse to eat when the wreck occurred.

As she sat down to wait for Pat to clean up, she saw yet another car stop down at the curb in front of the house.

"Not again," she muttered.

It's not what you think.

Sure enough, Millicent was right. The last person Tara would have expected to see walking up to the house was her nemesis, Prissy. Only Prissy wasn't alone. She was holding a little boy's hand, and he was crying.

"Oh no."

It's still not what you think. Stop expecting the worst and face it.

It wasn't often that Millicent called her down, so when she did, Tara knew enough to pay attention. As soon as they knocked, she reluctantly opened the door.

"Prissy . . . this is a surprise."

Prissy looked as uncomfortable as Tara felt. "I know. Hey, I saw you on TV. What you did after the tornado was amazing, and I'll tell you that we may not be friends, but I will never dis you again. I also want to tell you I'm so sorry about what happened to you and Flynn. I've been saying prayers that he gets well soon."

Tara blinked. This was the last thing she would have expected to come out of Prissy's mouth.

"This is good to know," Tara said, and then glanced down at the little boy. "Who's your friend?"

"My little brother, Raymond. He's seven, and he has a problem that I hope you can fix."

"Ah," Tara said. At least now the visit made sense. "Hi, Raymond. It's nice to meet you." She pointed at the object in the little boy's hand. "What do you have there?"

Raymond's eyes welled. "It's Wilson's leash." Then he hid his face against Prissy's leg and began to sob.

Prissy gave Tara a pleading look. "Wilson is Raymond's beagle. The meter reader left the gate to the back yard open today and he got out. We've been looking all afternoon and can't find him. Mom and Dad are still at work, and they're going to blame me for letting it happen. Like it's my fault the meter reader was a jerk. I know you don't owe me a thing, and I wouldn't ask it for myself, but I'd do pretty much anything for Raymond, even bug you when I know you pretty much hate my guts."

It was the honesty that sold Tara—that and the little guy's sobs.

"Can I hold the leash for a minute?" Tara asked.

Prissy handed it over, and the moment the leather touched Tara's palm, she saw the dog. The good part was that he wasn't already road kill, but he was curled up against a fence licking his leg, which made her think he could be hurt. She closed her eyes so she could concentrate on the surroundings through which it was moving.

"Can you see anything?" Prissy asked.

Tara's eyebrows knitted as she focused on the scene inside her mind.

"He's sitting against a fence licking his leg. He might have gotten hurt, which is why he didn't come home."

Prissy patted her little brother's back. "Don't cry, Raymond. Tara is helping us find Wilson, okay?"

He wiped the snot on his upper lip on the back of his sleeve. "Where is he?" Raymond asked.

Tara kept watching the scene unfold. In her head, it was like zooming out from the dog, to the sidewalk, then the houses, then to a street sign. When she saw a very familiar business, her eyes popped open. She had the location.

"He's in the alley next to Eskimo Joe's. The aroma of food

probably led him there. I don't know what's wrong with his leg, but I have the feeling that he can't walk on it."

Tara handed the leash back to Prissy, who was slack-jawed and staring in disbelief.

"How do you do that?" she whispered.

Tara shrugged. "I don't know. I was born this way." Then she knelt down. "You and your big sister will have Wilson home before you know it, okay?"

All of a sudden Raymond threw his arms around her neck. "Thank you for using your magic," he whispered.

Now Tara was the one with tears in her eyes. "You're welcome, Raymond. See you around, okay?"

Tara walked them to the door. "You should probably hurry. I didn't see anything bad happening, but to be on the safe side, the sooner he's in your car, the better."

Prissy paused. "Thanks, Tara. You are one serious lunatic, but I will defend your right to be whatever you need to be." Then she held out her hand. "Truce?"

"Truce," Tara said.

They shook on it.

She watched as the brother and sister headed back down the driveway at a fast pace. Raymond was talking non-stop as they drove away.

"Who was that?" Pat said, as he walked into the living room.

"Just a friend from school," Tara said. "So what are my choices?"

Pat grinned. "Besides Hideaway Pizza, Red Lobster is open. Mexico Joe's is open. Sonic Drive-In is open, and the Braum's Ice cream just off Western is open."

"Braum's. I want a chocolate malt and you like their bacon burgers. Is that okay with you?"

Pat gave her a quick, easy hug. "Honey, anything you want is okay with me. So, let's head that way, okay? I called Mona and told her I'd bring her something for supper when we came to visit. This will be perfect."

Chapter Ten

When Tara and her uncle walked into Braum's, the first thing the diners noticed were her bruises, then she saw their gazes shift to Pat. She heard their thoughts, wondering if it had happened in the tornado or if he had abused her. Even though it was the farthest thing from the truth, she hated that they would think that of him.

So don't let the assumption slide.

Tara blinked. Millicent's advice was so obvious she didn't know why she hadn't thought of it herself.

"I would like a large chocolate malt, Uncle Pat. I'm going to get a booth, okay?"

"Sure honey. Do you want anything else?"

"No, thank you. Just the malt."

Pat watched until she got to the booth then went to the counter to get in line.

Tara sat down and immediately smiled at the people sitting at the table just across the aisle.

"That looks good," she said. "Hot fudge sundae?"

The woman nodded as she stared at Tara's face even harder.

"I'm a mess, aren't I?" Tara said. "My boyfriend and I were in a wreck on Lakeview Road the other day. We went over the bridge into the water. I'm still pinching myself that I'm actually here ordering ice cream. I thought I was dead."

Her voice carried just enough to end the assumptions the people had been making, which was her intent.

The woman's expression shifted from suspicion to disbelief.

"Oh, my word, we saw that on the news the other night. Bless your heart. Is your boyfriend okay, too?"

"No, ma'am. He got hurt pretty bad. He's still in ICU, but

we think he's taken a turn for the better."

The woman smiled again as she and her husband got up from the table. "Glad you're doing okay. Have a nice evening, honey."

"You, too," Tara said. She eased herself to a more comfortable position and then caught the man in the booth in front of her staring.

He leaned forward, lowering his voice. "You're the girl who helped search and rescue after the tornado, aren't you?"

Here it comes, she thought, and nodded.

"My brother died that day."

Tara gave him a closer look. "You're Tom Lewis's brother, aren't you?"

His hands started to shake. "How did you know?"

"You look alike."

"Did you know him from before?"

"No sir. I only saw him that day after the storm."

"But he died in the storm. You couldn't have—"

Tara watched the reality of what she'd said appear on his face and she wanted him to understand that his brother was okay.

"He's the one who showed me where he was. He didn't want to cross over until his body had been found. I told him I would wait until the rescue people came, and that I would make sure they knew where to find his body. After that, he walked into the light."

The man's hands started to shake. "Lord have mercy. What a treasure you are, child. What a treasure."

He shook his head as he got up from the table, dumped the rest of his food in the trash, and then walked over to where Pat was standing in line.

Tara saw them talking, and then they shook hands. The man looked back at Tara one more time, and then walked out of the store. A couple of minutes later, Pat came to the booth and sat down.

"That man just bought our supper. He said to tell you, thank you for what you did for his brother."

Tara leaned back, then looked out the window, watching the man as he got in his car and drove away. It looked like he was crying.

"Maybe I was wrong, Uncle Pat."

"About what, honey?"

"People being weird about me. Maybe they don't all think that way, after all."

He grinned. "See. I told you it would be okay."

A woman behind the counter called out. "Pickup, order 223."

Pat glanced at his ticket. "That's us. Hang on, honey. I'll be right back."

Tara felt like she was standing outside of herself as she watched her uncle going back to the counter to pick up their food.

She could see all the other diners eating and talking, some laughing—a couple of them quietly fighting—but she imagined that they couldn't see her. In that moment a wave of déjà vu washed over her that left her reeling. It seemed that she'd been through times like this before—great worry and sadness, and yet an observer without ever participating—but in other centuries—as other people.

And then her uncle turned around. He was smiling as he carried the tray with their food back to the booth and just like that, the feeling passed and she was her sore and bruised self again, waiting for that chocolate malt to arrive.

"Here you go, honey, one chocolate malt for my best girl."

Tara smiled as he set the frosty cup in front of her, then tore the paper off her straw, poked it through the lid, and took her first sip. It was cold and sweet, and when she swallowed, the taste of chocolate stayed strong all the way down her throat.

"Taste good?" Pat asked, as he bit into his bacon burger.

She nodded and took another sip. All in all, it was turning out to be a better outing than she'd expected, and they finished eating without incident.

When Pat went back to pick up his to-go order for Mona, Tara headed to the bathroom. She locked the door behind her, used the bathroom and then quickly washed up, anxious to get to the hospital. She was drying her hands when someone rattled the knob.

Beware.

Tara froze. *Beware? Of who?*

Henry said to tell you that when you get out, throw an elbow and run.

Tara was in a panic. OMG. What was happening here?

Just do it.

She took a deep breath, readied her stance and swung the door inward. She caught a glimpse of a big woman and a flash of gaudy red hair as the woman lunged forward, grabbing Tara's forearm.

She threw her elbow up, and at the moment of contact, flashed on a face as she heard her grunt in pain. Tara pulled free of her grasp and ran up the narrow hall, hit the exit door with the flat of her hands and was outside and in the parking lot, running toward the car where her Uncle Pat waited.

She jumped inside and quickly locked the doors.

"Drive," she said breathlessly.

Pat looked wild-eyed. "What's wrong?"

"I don't know, but Millicent told me to run and I did. There's a big red-headed woman who keeps showing up everywhere I go, and I just saw her again. She grabbed me as I came out of the bathroom but I got away."

"I'm not driving away. I'm going to give that woman a—"

"No, Uncle Pat! Drive! Please!"

Pat was frowning as he put the car in gear, then backed out of the parking space and quickly drove away.

Tara looked back over her shoulder just as the woman came running out. She was holding her eye, and even though Tara couldn't hear her, she knew she was cursing. Tara also knew now that the woman wasn't stalking her to get her fortune read. This was the woman she'd seen in the picture with Sam Nettles and Michael O'Mara. She was definitely heavier and her hair was a different color, but there was no mistaking the fact that Tara had seen Michael O'Mara's face when the woman grabbed her arm.

Tara pulled out her cell phone and made a quick call to

Detective Rutherford. It didn't seem strange to her that she had his private number on her contact list. Her life was so lunatic that she really should have it on speed dial. When he answered, she relayed her info quickly.

"Detective Rutherford, this is Tara. You remember I told you about that woman in Sam Nettles' life?"

"Yeah. Don't tell me you know where she is?"

"At the Braum's just off Western, if you hurry?"

"How the hell, excuse my language, do you know this?"

"Because she tried to grab me as I came out of the bathroom. I gave her a bloody nose and ran. She was still there when we left, but I doubt she'll be there long."

"Did you see what she was driving?"

"No, but for the record, I realized it's not the first time I've seen her. I think she's been stalking me and I didn't know it."

"Go home and stay there."

"Nope. On the way to the hospital to see Flynn."

"Then don't leave there until you hear from me."

He hung up in her ear, which was fine with Tara. She'd delivered the message.

Pat took a deep breath as he braked for a red light. "You're being stalked?"

"I think so, but I didn't know it until just now."

"You've seen this woman before? When? Why didn't you tell me?"

"She started to come into my room the first night I was in the hospital. I thought she was just another nut wanting me to tell them lottery numbers or something, but she got freaked about something and left without asking me anything but my name."

"Good lord," Pat muttered.

"I thought I saw her once after that, and then the incident just now. But one good thing came from our contact."

"What's that?" Pat asked.

"I know for sure she had a relationship with the guy who kidnapped Flynn, which means she could have known about that hidden money. I'm pretty sure she's the person who killed

Sam's brother, Floy. I hope they catch her. If they do, that will mean Flynn and his mother won't be in danger anymore. Oh . . . and Detective Rutherford told us not to leave the hospital until we hear from him."

Pat muttered beneath his breath.

"What did you say?" Tara asked.

He sighed. "I was reminding myself about the promise I made to God when I found out you'd been hurt."

Tara frowned. "What did you promise?"

"That I would never take another drink as long as I lived if He'd just make sure you were all right."

Tara gasped. "Did you really, Uncle Pat?"

"Yes, honey, I did. And you may not have noticed, but there's not a drop of liquor left in the house. I poured it all down the drain the day I brought you home from the hospital. However, if you don't quit scaring years off my life, I may have to resort to something else to calm my nerves. I may have to take up knitting or whittling, or something equally embarrassing to stay sane around you."

Tara slid her hand across his arm. "That means a lot to me. I'm really proud of you," she said softly.

He grinned wryly. "Yeah, I'm pretty proud of myself, too. If we can just get you out of this latest mess and get Flynn well in the process, I'll be a happy man."

"Me, too, Uncle Pat. I know Flynn is waking up, but I'm so scared that he won't . . . that he will have . . ." She rubbed her face, as if trying to wipe away the bad thoughts. "That he won't be the same."

"I know, but at this point, Mona is willing to accept whatever his condition might be, as long as he lives through this."

Tara understood that. But she was thinking about what Flynn would accept, and she knew him well enough to know he would rebel in so many ways if he came back with physical or mental issues he couldn't control. Still, it was all out of their hands. At this point, all Tara could hope for was that the cops caught that crazy woman before she caught up with her.

French Langdon had traded his Harley for an SUV and was parked in the back of the Braum's parking lot, waiting for Tara and her uncle to emerge. He saw her uncle come out on his own and get in the car, then kept watching for Tara. But when she finally came out, he didn't expect to see a panicked expression on her face, or for her to be running.

He immediately started the car, uncertain what was about to go down. Then, just as they were about to drive away, he saw a big red-headed woman come running out of the store. She was holding her eye and cursing at the top of her lungs.

He grinned. Score one for the Luna chick again. And then he took a better look at the woman, past the god-awful red hair to her features.

"Well, I'll be a—"

He reached for his phone and hit a number on speed dial. "Boss. It's me. Guess who just crawled out from under a rock? May Schulter, sporting red hair and about a thirty-pound weight gain, but it's her. Want me to pick her up?"

His eyes narrowed as he listened for further orders. "Yeah, I can do that," he said shortly, and disconnected just as May Schulter made a run for her car.

When she drove out of the parking lot, French made it his business to follow. Not enough to make her suspicious, but close enough not to lose her. He was a little disappointed that he would no longer be tailing Tara Luna, but orders were orders. Besides, Tara would be a whole lot safer, now that they knew where the last piece to their puzzle was at.

Mona was alone in the waiting room when Pat and Tara arrived.

"We brought you some supper," Pat said, and handed her the sack with a Braum's burger and shake.

"You're both darlings to think of me," Mona said. "It's still a few minutes before visiting hours. Sit with me while I eat."

Tara sat, anxious to hear news of Flynn's progress, but she waited until Mona had taken a few bites before she began bombarding her with questions.

"Did he wake up yet?" Tara asked.

Mona shook her head. "No, but he's moving his arms and legs, which was a huge relief to all of us. The doctor didn't tell me at first, but they have been concerned that he could have suffered a spinal injury as well."

"Oh, my gosh, I'm glad I didn't know that or I would have really been freaking out," Tara said.

Mona nodded and then smiled at Pat, who offered her a handful of napkins.

"Also, I think he responds to my voice. When I talk to him, I can see his eyes moving beneath the lids. And once when I squeezed his hand, I felt a slight squeeze back."

"This is really good news, isn't it, Uncle Pat?"

"It sure is, but I'm worried about you, too, Mona. Have you gone home at all?"

"Yes. My sister has been staying with me. She comes through the day and stays so that I can go home and shower and get a little sleep. Although you can imagine how much sleep I actually get. I can't wait to get back here. I'm always afraid he'll wake up and call for me and I would be gone."

Pat glanced at Tara, remembering how fearful he'd been that he'd lose her, too.

"That's tough, but I definitely understand," he said.

"Is it okay if I go in with you when it's time?" Tara asked.

Mona smiled. "You go in by yourself, Tara. I think he'd like that."

Tara's vision blurred, but she blinked away the tears. No crying. Not while there was still hope for the best.

Detectives Rutherford and Allen and a couple of police cruisers arrived at Braum's, but it was too late. The red-headed woman was already gone. After talking to the work staff who remembered seeing her, and finding out they had a security camera overlooking the parking lot, the detectives were in a better frame of mind. The manager took them back to his office where they quickly viewed the last hour of footage.

They quickly spotted Tara Luna and her uncle's arrival, and within a minute of them going inside, they saw an older model, dark brown pickup pull into the parking lot and park close by. They watched a big, heavy-set woman get out. To their surprise, she walked over to Pat Carmichael's car, circled it slowly and wrote down the tag number before going inside.

A bus pulled out the lot, and a couple of other cars pulled in a few seconds later. One was a family with children, the other was a single driver in an SUV. They couldn't see his face, but when he parked at the back of the lot and didn't get out, they thought was strange.

They continued to watch the footage right up to the point where Tara's uncle came out alone and went to the car. A couple of minutes later, they saw Tara come running out of the store and jump into the car. As Tara and her uncle drove away, they saw the woman hurry out, then get into her old brown pickup and followed them.

"Well, that's it. There she goes," Detective Allen said. "And we can't get a clear view of her license tag in either shot."

"Wait!" Rutherford said, pointing to the SUV in the back of the lot. "There goes that SUV, too, and it looks to me as if he's following the both of them. What the hell, excuse my language, is going on here? Can you get an ID on that SUV? Yeah! There's the tag. Allen, run that number. I want to know what that Luna girl has got herself mixed up in now."

Tara kept a close watch on the clock, and when visiting time approached, she interrupted Pat and Mona's conversation.

"Uncle Pat. Mona. It's about time to go into ICU. I'm going to go wait at the door, okay?"

Pat frowned. "I'll walk you."

"Don't be silly. I'll be fine," Tara said.

Pat arched his eyebrows. "I'll walk you," he said again.

Tara sighed. Now that he knew about the woman who'd been stalking her, he wasn't going to let up.

Mona frowned. "Is everything okay?"

Tara smiled quickly to relieve Mona's mind. "Yes. It's just that ever since they outed my psychic self on TV, I've been getting harassed at every corner. Uncle Pat is just being protective."

"Good grief," Mona said.

"I'll be right back," Pat said.

He and Tara quickly left the waiting room and headed for ICU. "Sorry," he said. "But until they get that crazy redhead off the streets, you're not going anywhere on your own."

Tara nodded. She wasn't going to argue. She'd been a little freaked out by the whole thing herself. They reached ICU and joined the other people who were waiting to go in. When the doors opened a couple of minutes later, the visitors began to file in, two at a time.

Pat waved at Tara, and then headed back to Mona, leaving her to go in alone. Her heart was pounding as she walked toward Flynn's bed again. After all the stuff she'd heard about Flynn's progress, she was more hopeful for his future than she had been in days.

When she reached his bed, everything looked the same, right down to the beeping heart monitor and oxygen tube. She could smell the slight scent of shaving cream as she ran the back of her finger against his cheek. It was soft and smooth. Someone had been shaving him daily. It hurt her heart to think of him being unable to perform even this simple task.

She pulled a chair up beside his bed, taking a moment to look at the boy who had stolen her heart. He was at that in-between stage, when a boy begins looking like a man, and it was obvious what a handsome man he would be. His features were clean-cut, with a strong chin and a straight nose. His eyebrows were dark, the long lashes on his eyelids even darker. Tara loved the shape of his mouth, and loved it even more when he was kissing her. She wanted that Flynn back, but like Mona, she was ready to accept the one who woke up, regardless of how he came.

Blinking away tears, she slowly slid her hand beneath his

and gave his fingers a gentle squeeze.

"Hey you, it's me, Tara. I know you're back. I know you're getting stronger. And I know it's hard. I'm so proud of you. You keep fighting, okay?"

She squeezed his hand again to emphasize what she'd said, and right afterward, she felt a slight squeeze back.

OMG.

He was letting her know, in the only way he could, that he'd heard her.

"There are so many things I need to tell you. Some of it is about those men who kidnapped you. I think the police are about to figure out who killed Floy Nettles. Oh Flynn, I can't wait for the day when I see your pretty brown eyes looking at me again. Just don't give up. You're doing great."

Suddenly, he scratched his fingers on the sheet, as if to get her attention.

She patted his hand. "I see you. I know you're in there."

He slightly scratched the sheet again.

"Okay. I'm looking at your hand. What is it you want me to see?"

For a few seconds, he didn't move, and just when she thought he was gone again, he lifted a finger and very slowly traced the shape of a heart on the sheet beside her hand.

"Oh Flynn, I heart you, too," she whispered, then dropped her forehead against the bed rail as the tears rolled down her face.

Suddenly his hand was on the crown of her head, but even more shocking than the fact he'd moved it, she could actually feel his heartbeat. When hers suddenly skipped a beat and then picked up in rhythm to his, she bit her lip to keep from sobbing. She could feel every pain in his body and knew every fear in his mind. It was as if the two of them had become one heart—one mind—one body.

She reached for his hand, threading her fingers through it, and holding on until her warmth had permeated his skin.

"Do you feel that, Flynn? That's my heartbeat. Can you feel the rhythm? That's my joy, knowing that you're coming back.

Don't be afraid. Whatever you have to face when you wake up, you won't face it alone. Your mom will be with you. I will be with you. Your friends will be with you. We won't quit on you, Flynn, no matter what. Just open your eyes. Come back to us. Please."

Tara.

She froze. That wasn't Millicent's voice.

Tara.

When she heard it again, she stood up and began looking around, trying to find the source. Then she felt Flynn's fingers trying to tighten on her hand and looked down.

His eyelids were fluttering. She could see a muscle jerking at the side of his mouth. When she tried to pull back, his grip tightened.

OMG. Could that be Flynn she was hearing? Was that possible?

Is that you?

Yes.

Her heart skipped a beat. *I can hear you like I hear Millicent.*

I can hear you, too. I heard you calling, Moon Girl. You found me when I was lost. You brought me back.

Wake up, Flynn. Open your eyes.

His eyelids twitched again, making the dark lashes shading his eyes flutter like butterfly wings.

Tara held her breath. *I'm still here.*

So am I.

She watched his eyelids fluttering as they began to open. Breath caught at the back of her throat. She didn't know whether to go get a nurse, or witness the miracle alone.

Don't go.

And just like that, the decision was made for her. *I won't.*

His nostrils flared as he drew a deeper breath, and at the same time his forehead creased as the pain from the surgery and broken ribs shot through his body.

He groaned.

Her gaze was locked onto his face. "I know you hurt, Flynn. I'm so sorry, but you will get well."

When he stilled, she thought he had slipped back into unconsciousness. Then just like that, he opened his eyes.

She stood up so that she would be in his direct line of vision, and the moment she did, his gaze locked into hers. When he saw the scratches and bruises on her face, he licked his lips and frowned.

"Hurt you," he said softly.

"It's not so bad and neither are you," she whispered, and then leaned over the bed and kissed the side of his cheek. "I need to go tell the nurses that you're awake."

He slowly closed his eyes.

"I'll be back again," she said, but when she tried to turn loose of his hand he still held on. "What is it, Flynn?"

"Love," he said softly.

Tara closed her eyes. *Love you, too, Flynn O'Mara.*

The corner of his mouth tilted up just a little bit, indicating that he'd heard her, only she hadn't said that aloud. That was when Tara knew. Not only had Flynn come back to them, he *had* come back different, just not in the way that they'd feared. He would get well. But he would never be the way he'd been before. He'd come back like her.

She took a deep breath and then headed for the nurses' station.

"Flynn just woke up," she said softly. "He knew who I was, spoke a few words, then went back to sleep. There are five minutes left in the visiting time. May I please leave so his mother can come in?"

The nurse nodded.

Tara went out the door as the nurse went toward his bed. She headed for the waiting room and burst in on the run.

"He woke up! He woke up! The nurse said you could go in but you need to hurry. Time is almost up."

"Praise the lord," Mona cried, and ran out of the room.

Pat was on his feet as Tara walked into his arms. "Oh, Uncle Pat. He woke up and he knew me. He's going to get well."

Pat laughed. "That's the best news ever," he said and gave her a big hug.

Tara nodded. She wasn't going to give away the rest of the news. That would be for Flynn to tell—or not. If he chose to keep quiet about the fact that he could slip in and out of people's thoughts like a thief in the night, so be it. He would learn how to control it, just like she'd learned how to use what she could do.

"Come sit," Pat said. "I have news."

Tara sat down. "What happened?"

"Detective Rutherford came by. They caught up with the redhead, thanks to some help from an uncover agent for the OSBI."

Tara's mouth dropped. "Does that mean what I think it means?"

Pat grinned. "If you're thinking the Oklahoma State Bureau of Investigation, then yes. Anyway, he was assigned to locate the remaining members of a gang that had stolen a large amount of money that belonged to the Federal government."

"Michael O'Mara's so-called buried treasure?"

He nodded. "And that woman who's been harassing you, wanted you to help her find it. She thought because you were psychic that you could just wave a finger in the air and point her to it."

"Is she under arrest?"

"I believe the term is, "being questioned" about Floy Nettles' murder. It turns out she saw him talking to Flynn, thought Flynn might have told him where it was, then she got mad when he laughed in her face for thinking she was going to get a cut. At any rate, the OSBI agent assured the Stillwater P.D. that the redhead was the last member of the gang, and now that she is in custody, you, Mona and Flynn are safe."

"But no one knows where the money is," Tara said.

"That's their problem," Pat said.

"Right."

She was so relieved, and at the same time, still wired from the tension under which they'd been living. She leaned forward, resting her elbows on her knees as she stared at a stain on the floor. The gang's greed had caused so much misery. She was glad that was all behind them.

Like Flynn, Stillwater was still in recovery mode from the tornado. It would take many more months before homes could be rebuilt. Lives had been lost. Families had been forever changed. But the ones who'd been left behind owed it to the ones who'd died to live out the rest of their lives in the best ways they knew how. It was the least they could do and Tara was grateful her family and her friends families were part of those left behind.

A few moments later Mona came back, laughing and talking. As soon as she and Pat began to talk, Tara zoned out, tired, but happy. A few minutes later, she happened to look up and caught a man watching her from the hallway.

He smiled.

She stood up.

"Back in a minute," she said, and headed out the door. It was past time she and French Langdon talked face to face.

"Hey, tough stuff. Heard your boyfriend is coming around. Great news."

"Were you in school because of Flynn? Because you knew he might be in trouble?"

"So I didn't look young enough to be there on my own? Dang. That's gonna bite not being able to do that anymore."

"You're the one who pulled us out of the car, aren't you?"

He shrugged. "Right place. Right time."

"Thank you."

He smiled again, transforming the stern expression he usually wore. "You're welcome. Since I saved your life, I don't suppose I could guilt you into a date or anything like that."

Tara should have been shocked, but she could tell that teasing was part of his personality.

"No, I don't suppose you could."

His smile widened, which pulled his scar into an interesting crease down the side of his face. "You're too young for me, anyway."

"You're way too old for me," Tara said.

He laughed softly. "Thank goodness we avoided that disaster before it happened."

Tara grinned. He *was* funny and a little bit charming, but her heart belonged to Flynn.

French held out his hand. "So, let's just shake on it and go about our business, okay?"

The moment Tara touched his hand she flashed on a boat fire.

"Are you going on vacation?"

He looked a little startled. "Yeah, to the Bahamas . . . do a little deep sea fishing."

"Don't get on the boat. It's going to catch on fire."

His eyes narrowed. "How do you feel about my dad's bass boat and the family farm pond?"

"Good."

"Thanks for the heads up, Tara Luna. Since you just saved my life, I think we're even now, don't you?"

She nodded.

"Hey, your uncle is looking for you," he said, and pointed over her shoulder.

Tara turned around and saw Uncle Pat frowning. She smiled and waved, so he'd know not to worry, and when she turned back around, French Langdon was gone.

She looked up and down the hall but he was nowhere in sight. After a moment of disappointment, she let it go. They'd said all they needed to say.

He'd just made goodbye a little easier.

She headed back to the waiting room, confident that their lives were finally getting back on track, and thankful Flynn was going to be around to live it with her.

That night when she went to bed, the last thing she saw before she closed her eyes was the dream-catcher hanging over her bed.

She slept without dreaming, and then just before morning an all-too familiar face popped up in her dream.

The sky was clear—the ground solid, the grass was green beneath her feet. It was a far cry from the limbo they'd been lost in before. Tara felt a breeze upon her skin and turned to face it. It caught the hair hanging down around her shoulders and lifted it from her neck to cool her skin.

She closed her eyes, inhaling the sweet scents of flowers in bloom and when she opened them, Michael O'Mara was standing before her. He seemed a little younger, and less foreboding, but she knew why he'd come.

"You promised to help me talk to Flynn," he said.

"I know."

"Are you going to keep your promise?"

"Of course, but there's something you need to know. There's a possibility that he will be able to hear you on his own. He came back changed. He can hear people's thoughts."

"I know, but only the living. He will not have the connection with the dead that you do."

"Then I will be your voice."

"You will tell him the truth, even if it's something you think might hurt him?"

"I will deliver your message as you give it. When will you come?"

"I will pick the time. All you need to remember is that you have given your word."

Even though her feet weren't moving, Tara began to move backward. As she did, O'Mara grew smaller and smaller until he eventually disappeared.

Tara woke up.

She lay without moving, thinking about what O'Mara had said. It didn't have to mean there was anything bad going to happen again. It just meant that whatever it was he wanted Flynn to know might disappoint him, or hurt him emotionally. There was absolutely no reason to assume it had anything to do with physical danger.

No reason at all.

The End

Where did Tara's Adventures Begin?

My Lunatic Life

Excerpt

Four days later, the dark shadow came back.

It was three minutes after four in the morning when Tara woke up needing to go to the bathroom. She was on her way back to bed when she sensed she was no longer alone. Her heart skipped a beat as the darkness between her and the hallway moved into her room. A normal girl's first instinct would have been to scream or run away, but Tara was used to spooks. She stomped into her bedroom with her hand in the air.

"Look, Smokey . . . I'm bordering on PMS, so you don't want to mess with me. State your business or make yourself scarce. And don't go *through* me again to do it. I'll tell Henry and Millicent to kick your behind so hard you'll never be able to put two ectoplasmic molecules together again. Do you read me?"

The shadow shifted then disappeared through the floor.

"That's better," Tara muttered, then headed to the dresser, where she'd left her jewelry box. She dug through it until she found her Saint Benedict's medal, fastened the chain around her neck, and then crawled back into bed. "Like I don't already have enough to deal with," she said wearily, then punched her pillow a couple of times before settling back to sleep.

All too soon, the alarm was going off and another strange

day was in motion.

The first week at school sped by without further trouble. At home, Uncle Pat got cable hooked up to the TV and internet to Tara's laptop. She caught up on episodes of *Glee* and *Gossip Girl*. She was beginning to believe everything was smoothing out. Then week two came, reminding her she was still the new kid in school.

Tara was on her way to first period when she turned a corner in the hall and came up on the cheerleader trio who she now thought of as The Blonde Mafia. Prissy saw Tara, then pointed at her and said something that sent the other two into a fit of giggles.

"You are so lame. You're almost as funny as your name," Prissy said, as Tara walked past.

Tara rolled her eyes. "Is that rhyme supposed to pass for white girl rap?"

Prissy's face flushed angrily as kids standing nearby heard it go down and started laughing, but Tara didn't hang around for a second stanza. She didn't have time for their petty crap. She walked about ten feet further down the hall when she heard a shriek and turned just in time to see two hanks of Prissy's hair suddenly standing straight up on either side of her face like donkey ears.

Millicent! Tara stifled a grin. "I knew that was gonna happen," she said, and kept on walking.

Tara's first-period teacher was at her desk, poking frantically at the screen of her smart phone. She looked up when Tara walked in, nodded distractedly, then returned to what she'd been doing. The air was so thick with distress that Tara immediately sensed what was wrong.

Mrs. Farmer had money troubles.

That was something she understood. She and Uncle Pat rarely had an excess of the green stuff, themselves. And considering that his new job with the city of Stillwater involved reading electric meters, they weren't going to get rich this year, either.

She slipped into her seat, then took her book out of her backpack, trying to concentrate on something besides the misery Mrs. Farmer was projecting. But for a psychic, it was like trying to ignore the water while going through a car wash. Tara was inundated with wave after wave of her teacher's thoughts and emotions.

All of a sudden she knew Mrs. Farmer's husband drank too much. Her mother was a nag. Her sister was married to a doctor, which made her own husband's problems seem even worse. And suddenly Tara knew something Mrs. Farmer did not.

It wasn't that Mrs. Farmer couldn't manage her money. *Someone was stealing it.*

The room began to fill with other students, and a few minutes later the bell rang, signaling the beginning of class. Tara felt Mrs. Farmer trying to focus on her job and Tara tried to do the same. English was one of her favorite classes.

"Good morning," Mrs. Farmer said. "Your assignment over the weekend was to read the poem, *The Female of the Species,* by Rudyard Kipling, then write a one-hundred word paper on it. This morning we're going to read your papers aloud in class."

The collective groan that followed her announcement was no surprise. Tara sensed that half the class hadn't even read the poem and of the ones who had, less than a dozen had completed the assignment. Tara pulled out her notes but had a difficult time focusing. She kept keying in on Mrs. Farmer's plight.

She knew what needed to be done to help her, but it meant making herself vulnerable.

The hour passed, and when the bell rang students scattered, even as Mrs. Farmer was still giving them their assignment for tomorrow. Tara had argued with herself all through class, when she really hadn't had an option. If she'd seen someone stealing, she would have told. Knowing it was happening and who was doing it and not telling was the same thing to her. She waited until the last of the students were gone, then headed toward the front of the room, where her teacher was erasing the blackboard.

"Mrs. Farmer, may I speak with you a minute?"

Unaware anyone had lingered behind, Mrs. Farmer whirled around, startled. "Oh, my. You startled me, dear. I didn't know anyone was still here. You're Tara, right?"

"Yes, ma'am." Tara sighed. There was nothing to do but jump in with both feet. "I need to ask you something, and then I need to *tell* you something."

She could see the confusion on her teacher's face, but she had to hurry or she'd be late for second period.

"Who's Carla?" Tara asked.

"Why . . . that's my babysitter," Mrs. Farmer said. "She stays at my home during the day and takes care of my twin daughters. They're only three."

"Okay . . . I need to tell you that she's stealing money from you. She's taking blank checks out of the new pads of checks in the box and forging your signature. That's why you're account stays overdrawn."

Tara could see all the color fade from her teacher's face. Mrs. Farmer gasped. "How do you know this?"

Tara sighed. "I just do, okay?"

Mrs. Farmer grabbed her by the arm. "Do you know Carla Holloway? Did she *tell* you this?"

"No, ma'am. I asked you who Carla is, remember? Uncle Pat and I just moved here, remember? We really don't know anyone."

"Then how . . ."

"Maybe I'm psychic, okay? When you go home this evening, get out your new checks and look through the pads. You'll find a couple of checks will be missing from each one. Confront Carla. She'll fold. And don't forgive her to the point of letting her keep babysitting for you . . . because she's using the money to buy drugs."

"Oh dear Lord," Mrs. Farmer gasped, and reached for her cell phone.

Tara ducked her head and made a run for the hall. She'd done all she could do. The rest was up to Mrs. Farmer.

She made it to second period just as the last bell rang. That teacher frowned as she slid into her seat. Tara heard a soft masculine whisper from behind her.

"Good save, Moon girl."

She turned. Flynn O'Mara grinned at her. Tara rolled her eyes and then dug her book out of her backpack, trying not to think about how stinkin' cute Flynn was. Kind of had that classic heartthrob look, but with more muscles and straighter hair.

Henry showed up about fifteen minutes later and began trying to get Tara's attention. She sent him mental signals to be quiet, but he wasn't getting the message. Just before class ended they heard a loud commotion out in the hall. It sounded like doors banging—dozens of doors—against the walls. Henry threw up his hands and vaporized. That's when she realized whatever was going on out in the hall might have something to do with Millicent. The door to her classroom opened and flew back against the wall with a loud bang. The fact that it seemed to have opened by itself was not lost on the teacher or the students.

"Wait here!" the teacher cried, and dashed out into the hall.

Moments later Tara heard the fire alarm go off. The teacher came running back into the room.

"Walk in an orderly line and follow me!" Students grabbed backpacks and folders and fell into line behind her as she strode quickly out the door.

Tara's stomach sank as she slid in between Flynn O'Mara and a girl with blue hair.

"It's probably nothing," Flynn said over her shoulder.

Tara shivered. She knew better. It was something all right. It was Millicent. But why?

The halls grew crowded as students filed out of the classroom and made for the exits. To their credit, the exodus was somewhat orderly. As soon as they reached the school grounds, security guards began directing them to the appropriate areas. In the distance, Tara could hear sirens.

She kept looking back toward the school building. What had Millicent done?

Henry appeared in front of her, as if to say *I told you so*, then disappeared just as quickly again. A pair of fire trucks pulled into the school yard. Firemen jumped down from the rigs and hurried into the building. As Tara watched, smoke began to pour out of one of the windows on the second floor.

OMG! Millicent had set the school on fire? Why would Tara's lifelong ghost pal set the school on fire?

The moment she thought it, Tara heard Millicent's voice in her head.

I didn't set the fire. It was already burning between the walls. Give me a break. I was trying to help.

Sorry, Tara told her.

As if that wasn't enough drama for the day, a loud rumble of thunder suddenly sounded overhead.

Ghosts couldn't control the weather, so this wasn't Henry or Millicent's doing. A strong gust of wind suddenly funneled between the school and the gym. She shuddered. Even though the day was warm, that wind gust was chilly. Then it thundered again. She looked up at the underside of the building storm clouds, frowning at how dark they were getting.

"Are you cold?" Flynn asked.

She turned to find him standing right behind her.

"A little. Who knew we'd need jackets today? It was in the nineties when I left home this morning."

"Take mine," he said, as he slipped out of his denim jacket and then put it over her shoulders.

"Then you'll be cold," she said.

"Nah. I'm good."

She slipped the jacket on. The warmth from his body still lingered in the fabric, giving her a momentary impression of how it would feel to have his arms around her. It was an image that made her blush.

The wind continued to rise, with thunder rumbling every few minutes.

Tara shivered nervously as she looked up at the clouds. She hated storms.

"We're going to get soaked," she muttered.

A shaft of lightning suddenly snaked out of the clouds and struck nearby, sending the crowd into a panic.

"Into the gym!" Coach Jones yelled.

He waved his arms and pushed kids toward the gym.

"To the gymnasium!" a teacher echoed, and the crowd began to move. When the next shaft of lightning struck, this time in the football field nearby, they began to run. And then the rain came down.

Tara ran as hard as everyone else, but the ground was getting muddy and more than once she lost traction and slipped. If she fell, she would get trampled before anyone knew she was even down there. No sooner had the thought gone through her mind than her feet went out from under her. She was falling and all she could see were the legs of hundreds of students aiming straight for her.

Suddenly, Flynn pulled her upright. "Hang on to me, Moon Girl!"

She grabbed hold of his hand. Together they made it into the gym. They were heading for the bleachers before they realized they were still holding hands. They turned loose of each other too quickly, then grinned for being so silly.

"Thanks for your help," she said, and took off his jacket. "It's soaked. Sorry."

"It'll dry. Are you okay?"

"Yeah. Sure. Thanks again."

He eyed the dark hair plastered to her head and the wet t-shirt she was wearing as his grin widened. "You might wanna keep that jacket for a while." She looked down, then rolled her eyes. Everything—and she did mean, everything—showed, right down to her blue bra and the little mole next to her belly button.

"Perfect," Tara muttered. "Just perfect."

"Yeah. I agree," Flynn said.

She thumped him on the arm and then crossed her arms across her chest.

"Stop looking," she hissed.

"I'm trying, but hey . . . don't blame me for an appreciation of the finer things in life."

Tara laughed despite herself, then put his jacket back on and climbed the bleachers. She sat down a little away from a crowd of sophomores and began wringing the water out of her hair.

I like her, Flynn thought. *I like this crazy girl.*

Flynn paused. If he followed her up and sat down beside her, it would only intensify what he was already feeling. There was no pretense with her. She was a little odd and definitely different from the other girls in school, but he had plans for his last year of high school that didn't include getting messed up by another female. Bethany Fanning had done it to him big time over the summer, and he wasn't in the mood to go through another dose of female drama. Still, something told him that Tara Luna wasn't fake, and if there *was* drama in her life, she wasn't the kind to exaggerate it.

He felt someone push him toward her, but when he turned around, there was no one there. Frowning, he climbed the bleachers and then plopped down right in front of her. That way he was close, but not staking out territory.

Tara had seen Millicent give Flynn a push. So, Millicent wasn't satisfied with playing havoc at school today. Now she was playing matchmaker.

I delivered him. You do the rest.

"I can do just fine on my own, thank you," Tara said beneath her breath.

Flynn frowned. "Sorry. I didn't know you'd set up boundaries. Want me to move?"

"No. No. Not you. I wasn't talking to you. Sit here . . . wherever you want. Sorry."

Flynn's frown deepened as he looked around. "Then who were you talking to, if not to me?"

"Ghosts," Tara said. "I was talking to ghosts."

"Yeah, right. Whatever. I can take a hint." He got up and moved away.

Now see what you did.

"Just stop meddling," Tara snapped.

Whatever, Millicent said, echoing Flynn, then made herself scarce.

Tara slumped. Could this day possibly get any worse?

And Next...

The Lunatic Detective

Excerpt

Chapter One

Worms crawled between the eye sockets and over what had once been the bridge of her nose. The lower jaw had come loose from the joint and was drooping toward the breastbone, as if in eternal shock for the circumstance. The finger bones were curled as if she'd died in the middle of trying to dig her way out.

Tara stood above the newly opened grave, staring down in horror.

"Is that you, DeeDee?"

But DeeDee couldn't answer. There was the problem with her jaw.

All of a sudden, someone pushed Tara forward and she felt herself falling . . . falling . . . into the open grave . . . on top of what was left of poor DeeDee Broyles.

That was when she screamed.

Tara Luna sat straight up in bed, the sheet clutched beneath her chin as she stared wild-eyed around her bedroom, her heart pounding against her ribcage like a drum. All of a sudden, the loud roar of an engine swept past her window.

VVRRROOOMMM! VVRROOOMMM!!

She flinched, then relaxed when she saw the familiar silhouette of her uncle, Patrick Carmichael. She glanced at the clock and groaned in disbelief as the roar of a lawn mower passed beneath her bedroom window again. It was just after eight a.m.—on a Saturday! Couldn't he have waited a little longer before starting that thing up?

I think you'd look great as a red-head.

Tara rolled her eyes. Millicent! She'd just had the worst dream ever and was not in the mood for any input on hairstyles from the female ghost with whom she shared her life.

"I am not dying my hair." She swung her legs over the side of the bed and stood up.

I was once a red-head . . . and a blonde . . . and a brunette.

Tara arched an eyebrow, but resisted commenting. She'd always suspected Millicent had been quite a swinger in her day because she was still way too focused on men.

"I'm going to shower," Tara announced, and headed for the bathroom across the hall. She opened the door just as Henry, the other ghost who shared her world, came floating by. Before she could stop herself, she'd walked through him.

She swiped at her face. "Eww! Henry! I hate when that happens!"

Henry didn't appear too pleased with her either, and vaporized himself in a huff.

He doesn't like to be displaced.

"Yeah, well I don't like to be slapped in the face with frozen spider webs, and that's what that feels like."

Interesting. I remember once when I was in France—

"Millicent. Please? I just woke up here."

A pinkish tinge suddenly flashed across Tara's line of vision, then she heard a very faint pop before Millicent's voice disappeared. "Oh great. Now she's ticked, too."

Still, finally glad to be alone, Tara closed the bathroom door behind her. Just because Henry and Millicent were no longer alive in the strict sense of the word, didn't mean she wanted them as company while she showered.

A short while later, she emerged, wide-awake and starving.

She dashed across the hall to her room, and dressed quickly in a pair of sweats and a new white tee from Stillwater, Oklahoma's world famous burger joint, Eskimo Joe's.

As she entered the kitchen, it was obvious from the dirty dishes in the sink that Uncle Pat had already cooked breakfast. She began poking around, hoping he'd left some for her, and hoping it was regular food and not one of his experiments.

Her uncle had a tendency to mix things that didn't necessarily go together. It was, he claimed, his way of 'going green' by not wasting perfectly good food. If she could only convince him to quit stirring everything into one big pot to heat it up, she would be happy. She didn't mind leftovers. She just wanted to know what it used to be before she put it in her mouth.

As she passed by the sink, she saw a shot glass sitting inside a cereal bowl and stopped. This wasn't good. If Uncle Pat had already started drinking this early in the morning, the day was bound to go to hell before dark. Still, after she found a plate of food in the microwave that actually looked good, her mood lightened a little. She could smell sausage and potatoes, which went well together. She just hoped the yellow stuff on the side was scrambled eggs. He'd been known to try and pass off mashed squash on her before, claiming eggs and squash were both yellow and fluffy, so he failed to see her issue. She poked her finger into the food. It had the consistency of eggs. She licked her finger, then grinned. Eggs!

"Bingo! Lucked out on this one." She popped it in the microwave to heat and poured herself a glass of juice.

With the first couple of months of her senior year at a new school behind her, she was beginning to feel like she belonged. She'd gotten off on the wrong foot with one of the cheerleaders, which had resulted in some pretty hateful gossip and hazing. When that had started, Millicent had felt an obligation to retaliate on Tara's behalf. Flying dishes and ink pens had then shifted the gossip about Tara at Stillwater High to an all-out accusation that Tara Luna was not just a lunatic, but also a witch. She could handle being both a psychic and a medium, but a witch? How lame was that?

As she dug into her breakfast, she couldn't help thinking about the one-eighty her life had taken after she'd used her psychic powers to figure out who had kidnapped Bethany Fanning, the head cheerleader of Stillwater High School. With the help of her new boyfriend, Flynn, and Bethany's boyfriend, Davis, they had managed to rescue Bethany just before she became fish food in Boomer Lake.

Just thinking about Flynn O'Mara made her shiver. He was one smooth hottie.

All in all, it had been an eventful two months.

She was still eating when she sensed she was no longer alone. Since the sound of the mower was still going strong, it couldn't be Uncle Pat. She could also sense that whoever was here wasn't mortal. She looked over her shoulder. When she saw the sad little ghost who'd come with the house they were renting, she sighed and pointed to a chair on the opposite side of the table.

"Hey, DeeDee. Have a seat. I had a dream about you last night. I've been waiting for you to come back. We need to talk."

DeeDee drifted past the chair Tara had indicated, choosing instead to hover near the doorway.

"Okay, here's the deal," Tara said, as she chewed. "Millicent explained your situation to me. I know you used to live in this house. I know you were also murdered here. I also know there was never an investigation into your murder because no one reported you missing . . . which leads me to the question, why not?"

DeeDee didn't have an answer. With a ghost, that usually meant she didn't know it. Spirits were often confused after they died. Sometimes they didn't understand what had happened to them, or where they were supposed to be. Tara knew that after the traditional 'passing into the light' they could come back and forth if they wished. But she suspected DeeDee had never crossed over. Ever. Which she found really sad.

"I'm really sorry that I don't have any answers for you, yet. But you already know I'm having problems with your brother,

Emmit."

When DeeDee suddenly went from passive to a dark, angry shadow, Tara flinched. Talk about being in a mood. DeeDee was certainly in one now.

"So, what do you suggest?" Tara asked.

The dark shadow swirled to the ceiling and then down to the floor, like a puppet dancing on a string.

"That is not a helpful answer," Tara muttered, and scooped another bite into her mouth, her eyes narrowing thoughtfully as she chewed. "Here's the deal. I've already done a lot of legwork on this mystery. I found out you and Emmit once owned this house together, although he totally denies he ever had a sister."

At that news, the dark shadow bounced from one end of the kitchen to the other, rattling dishes in the cabinets.

"Easy," Tara cautioned. "No breaking dishes, please. I also found out where he lives now. You know I went to see him, which opened up this huge can of worms. Something I said to him set him off in a big way because now he's stalking me."

The dark shadow shifted back to DeeDee's ghost again, drifting about a foot above the floor like dandelion puffs floating in the wind.

"But you already knew that, too, so don't play dumb," Tara muttered. "And, thank you again for scaring him off before he found me here the other day." She frowned. "However, I still can't figure out how he got a key to this house. There's no way the lock on the front door is still the one from back when you guys owned the house. Your freaky brother either picked the lock, or had some kind of master key. Either way, he scared the you-know-what out of me . . . digging through all our closets and stuff. I don't even want to think about what he would have done to me if he'd found me hiding in the back of Uncle Pat's closet. Like I said before, I owe you for scaring him off like that. But!" She pointed her fork at DeeDee. "Did you know he's stalking me outside of the house, too?"

Tara felt the little ghost's empathy as if she'd been hugged. "Yes, well, I'm sorry, too. Thanks to you and Millicent, I've managed to get away from him both times, but my luck can't hold forever. If only you could tell me where your body is buried, it would open an investigation, and the guilty party, whom I suspect is your brother Emmit, would be caught."

Like before, an image of upturned earth and a pile of leaves flashed through Tara's mind.

"Okay. I get that the killer dug a hole, and that it was probably in the fall, because there were leaves all over the ground. But where? No. Wait. I know you were buried in the back yard." Then she grimaced. "Imagine my joy in learning that. What I meant was, I don't know where in the back yard."

Another image of the backyard flashed in Tara's mind. It was like looking at a postcard someone had sent her. In this instance, the postcard had come from DeeDee.

"I already know it's in our backyard. But it's huge. I can't just start digging holes. I don't know how deep the hole was where you were buried, or where to start looking."

Sadness swept through Tara so fast that she was crying before she knew it.

"Oh, DeeDee," Tara whispered, as she swiped at the tears on her cheeks. "I'm not giving up. I'm just talking out loud."

Within the space of a heartbeat, she found herself alone.

"Bummer," Tara muttered. "What a way to start the weekend."

She glanced down at her plate. The food was not only cold, but after the interlude with DeeDee, Tara had lost her appetite. She carried her plate to the sink, ran the leftovers through the garbage disposal, and put her plate and the rest of the dirty dishes into the dishwasher. Then she waved at her uncle, who was passing by the window again. After that, she turned, put her hands on her hips and frowned.

"Time to get down to business. There's laundry to do. The floors need sweeping and I need to make a grocery list."

Tara didn't feel sorry for herself. Her life was her life. She didn't remember anything else. She had no memory of her parents, who'd died in a car wreck before her first birthday. Her family consisted of her and Patrick Carmichael, her mother's brother—a fifty-something bachelor with an itchy foot and a gypsy soul. They'd lived in so many different states during the seventeen years of Tara's life that she'd lost count. Except for his tendency to drink too much, too often, he was a good man and good to her.

They moved to Stillwater just before the beginning of school, and if Tara had anything to do with it, they would still be here when she graduated high school next year, and still here for the ensuing four or five years it would take for her to graduate college. Oklahoma State University was one of the best universities in the state, and it just happened to be right here in town.

The possibility they might not move again so soon was better than usual because her Uncle Pat had gone sweet on a waitress at Eskimo Joe's. The waitress just happened to be her boyfriend's mother, Mona, which was a little creepy, but there was nothing Tara could do about that.

The morning passed quickly as Tara finished cleaning house. Her uncle came inside at mid-morning and helped with the laundry. They'd done it together so many times that they had their own routine.

The last load of laundry was drying and Tara was mopping the last strip of floor when Pat came back into the kitchen.

"If you make out a grocery list, I'll do the shopping," he offered.

"Yay!" Tara said. She hated grocery shopping. "Give me a couple of minutes to finish up here and I'll get right to it."

"I'll be outside," Pat said. "I need to clean out the trunk of the car anyway."

"Okay," Tara said, as she put up the mop.

She went back to the counter and picked up the list that they'd started earlier in the week and began sorting through the pantry and the refrigerator, making notes of the things that needed to be replaced while absently dancing to a little Katy Perry playing on her iPod.

The front door had barely shut behind her uncle before Millicent popped up.

You're out of shampoo.

Tara looked up from the list and frowned. "And you know this because?"

There was a small accident in the bathtub.

Tara dropped the list onto the kitchen table. "Dang it, Millicent. Have you been making bubbles again?" She stomped off to the bathroom, muttering under her breath as she went. "I don't know why you persist in this when you know good and well you can't do bubble baths anymore."

Tara squealed as she ran into the bathroom, turned off the water running into the tub, then pulled the plug to let it run out. Of course, it was too late to stop what had already overflowed.

"Look at the mess you've made!" she shrieked. "You explain all this to Uncle Pat, will you? This stuff costs money, and we're not rolling in it, in case you've noticed."

Money? Isn't that what you got for finding that blonde bimbo?

Tara ignored the remark regarding the reward she'd gotten for finding Bethany Fanning, because that was going to be her ticket to four years of college. She sighed as she surveyed the partially flooded bathroom floor.

"I hope you're happy. I had just mopped this."

Sarcasm does not become you.

Tara knew her little ghost was gone, even before the sound of Millicent's voice disappeared.

"Henry! Why didn't you warn me?" Tara wailed, as she went to get the mop and bucket again.

Henry manifested long enough to blow her a kiss, then vaporized.

Tara wasn't amused. It seemed everyone had a place to be but her. She finished cleaning up the bathroom—again—and ran back to get the list before her uncle came back. She didn't want to explain why she was mopping the bathroom twice. Even though he'd finally accepted the fact that she was as psychic as the other women in his family had been, he didn't like to dwell on it.

She added a couple of other items to the list and hurried outside, only to find him engrossed in a conversation on his cell phone. From the laughter in his voice and the little she could hear, she guessed he was talking to Mona. When he saw Tara, he quickly said goodbye and stood.

"Got the list?" he asked.

Tara slipped it in his hand. "Are you going out with Mona tonight?"

He blushed. "I don't know . . . I might. Is there a problem?"

Tara sighed. "Flynn and I are going bowling."

"That's great," he said.

Tara shrugged. "You don't think it's weird? I mean, I'm going out with Flynn and you're dating his Mom?"

Pat frowned. "I fail to see the problem. I'm just taking a woman to dinner. We're not getting married. Flynn's not going to turn into your step-brother overnight."

"Ew! Ew! I hope not!" Tara cried. "How wrong would that be? All of us living under the same roof?"

Pat hugged her. "Honey, that is so far down the road of ever happening that you need to calm down. Dinner and a movie is not forever after, okay?"

Tara sighed. "Yeah, okay."

"So, I'll be back in a couple of hours. Kick back and take a good rest. I've got the back yard all cleaned up, but I've been thinking about putting in a small mum garden. You know . . . they're colorful and hardy and good to plant this time of year. Why don't you poke around and figure out a good place for us to plant them?"

Tara immediately thought of DeeDee. "Great idea, Uncle Pat. I'll do that."

He tweaked the end of her nose, then winked. "Okay. I'm leaving now. Later gator."

Tara rolled her eyes as he got in the car and drove away. Uncle Pat was a hoot with his funny old-time sayings.

Where are you planning to dig first?

Tara rolled her eyes. "Here's the deal, Millicent. It's not like you can just start digging holes. Our landlord would toss us out for tearing stuff up."

Tara went back into the house and locked the door firmly behind her as Millicent continued.

Then how are you going to find DeeDee?

"I don't know, okay? I'm going outside now, and if I'm real lucky, DeeDee will pop up, point her little ghostly finger and say 'X marks the spot.'"

As I have stated before, sarcasm does not become you.

Tara sighed. Great start to her Saturday. She'd displaced some of Henry's molecules, ticked Millicent off, and made DeeDee sad. And that was only the ghost side of her troubles. Uncle Pat had a date with Flynn's mom. What if there was hugging and kissing involved? What if they actually hooked up?

OMG. OMG.

Her feet were dragging as she headed out the back door, then paused on the bottom porch step with her hands on her hips.

"Okay. If I wanted to hide a body out here, where would it be?"

A picture popped into her head and she realized it was another 'postcard' from DeeDee. Just as she started to dismiss it, she realized what she was seeing wasn't what the back yard looked like now. It was different. Decidedly different. The back yard fence wasn't chain link, it was wood, and roses were climbing up the trellises against it. There was a circle of irises around a birdhouse on a pole, and a vegetable garden in the far north end. And there were morning glory vines all over the side of a shed that was no longer here.

OMG. DeeDee was showing her what the back yard used to look like.

"Okay, DeeDee! I get it. Keep it coming. I see it. Trees. There were big shade trees. And before you showed me a pile of leaves. I remember. I remember."

Tara leaped off the step and started out across the yard, following the old stone path that wound through the yard. Now the path even made sense. It had led to different parts of the garden.

As she walked, she couldn't imagine the depths of depravity it would take to kill someone, let alone a member of your family. And even though she didn't know who had killed DeeDee

Broyles, her brother seemed the obvious culprit. He had denied ever having a sister, then broke into Tara's house and was still stalking her. It wasn't looking good for Emmit.

She wondered what the prison system did with old men like him. Was there a senior citizens wing in the penitentiary? Did they still draw Social Security and get retirement checks? How weird was that?

Tara was lost in thought as she followed the path, trying to figure out where someone could dig a hole big enough to hide a body and make sure no one found it when she realized she'd been looking at the answer all the time.

The fence. It used to be tall. Wood. All around the yard. No one could see over. No one could see through.

OMG. You could dig holes all over and no one would know it. You'd have all the time in the world to plant bushes or shrubs, or anything you wanted to hide the fact that earth had been overturned.

She stopped, put her hands on her hips and turned around, looking back toward the house. Uncle Pat wanted her to find a place to plant some mums. She wanted to find a body. Both required digging holes. Piece of cake.

Henry suddenly popped up in front of her, waving his hands.

Tara frowned. "What's up? Don't tell me Millicent is making bubbles in the bathtub again? No? Uncle Pat? Something happened to Uncle Pat?"

I think he's trying to tell you someone's coming down the alley.

Millicent's explanation wasn't warning enough. Tara pivoted just in time to see a car coming down the alley between the houses. No one was supposed to drive through there except maybe city employees. Then she realized she'd seen that car before—and the man driving it.

It was Emmit Broyles.

Oh crap! He was doing it again. He was still stalking her.

She started to run toward the house, when she realized it would give away the fact that she was scared of him. So far, Emmit didn't know she was on to him. She remembered reading once that the best defense was an offense so she lifted her hand and started waving as she moved toward the alley.

"Hi, Mr. Broyles," she cried, and jogged toward the fence, as if expecting him to stop.

The look on his face was priceless. His bushy white eyebrows shot upward as if someone had tied strings to them and given them a yank. He must have tried to stomp on the accelerator, but he was obviously distracted enough that he missed and stomped the brake instead.

All of a sudden he was flying forward. His chin hit the steering wheel and the hat he'd been wearing shot off his head and landed on the dash.

"Are you all right?" Tara yelled, as she neared the fence.

Even though all the windows were up, she could tell he was cursing at the top of his voice. He grabbed his hat, shoved it back on his head. Ignoring the blood dripping from his chin, he finally found the accelerator and roared off down the alley.

Tara grinned.

I think that went well.

Tara's smile widened. "Yeah, it did, didn't it?"

She turned around to go back to the house only to realize DeeDee was standing right beside her.

"Oh. Man. You did it again, didn't you?" Tara asked.

DeeDee disappeared.

"So, obviously we're not discussing this."

How would you feel if your brother was the one who ended your life?

Tara's smile died. "I never thought about that."

Because you never had a brother?

"No. Because I didn't think how DeeDee would take the news. I guess I just assumed they didn't get along."

You know what they say about assume. It makes an—

"Yes, yes, I know. An ass out of u and me. Very funny."

Tara heard the phone ring and sprinted toward the house. She was slightly out of breath when she answered.

"Hello?"

"Hey, Moon girl, I must be getting better by the minute. The mere sound of my voice has left you breathless."

Tara laughed out loud. "You are too funny," she said. "I was in the back yard looking for . . . uh . . . I was in the back yard."

"So, are we still on for tonight?" Flynn asked.

"Absolutely," Tara said. "We're going bowling, right?"

"Yeah, unless you'd rather do something else?"

"No. No. I love to bowl. I'm not very good, but it's fun."

"Good. How about some Hideaway pizza before we go?"

"Oh, yum! I've heard they make the best."

"Oh, yeah," Flynn said. "So I'll pick you up about six, okay?"

"Yes."

Tara started to hang up, then thought of his mom and her uncle. "Hey, Flynn?"

"Yeah?"

"Did you know your mom and Uncle Pat have a date tonight, too?"

There was a moment of silence. Then a chuckle. "No, but I'm cool with it. Aren't you?"

"Oh, it's not that. It's just . . . kind of weird."

"You think too much, Moon girl. Let the old folks have their fun."

Tara laughed. "See you at six."

About Sharon Sala

Sharon Sala's stories are often dark, dealing with the realities of this world, and yet she's able to weave hope and love within the words for the readers who clamor for her latest works.

Her books repeatedly make the big lists, including The New York *Times*, *USA Today*, and *Publisher's Weekly*, and she's been nominated for a RITA seven times, which is the romance writer's equivalent of having an OSCAR or an EMMY nomination. Always an optimist in the face of bad times, many of the stories she writes come to her in dreams, but there's nothing fanciful about her work. She puts her faith in God, still trusts in love and the belief that, no matter what, everything comes full circle.

Visit her at sharonsalabooks.com and on Facebook.

CPSIA information can be obtained
at www.ICGtesting.com
Printed in the USA
LVOW08s0006150317

527246LV00001B/59/P